The Book of Emma

Also by the author

Novels:
La Dot de Sara
Le Livre d'Emma (published by Les Éditions du remue-ménage)
Un Alligator nomme Rosa

Short Stories:
Le Silence comme le sang

Poetry:
Balafres

Books for young people:
Alexis d'Haïti
Le Noël de Maïté
Alexis, fils de Raphaël
Vingt petits pas vers Maria

Haitian Folktales:
L'oranger magique: conte d'Haïti
La légende du poisson amoureux

The Book of Emma

Marie-Célie Agnant
translated by Zilpha Ellis

INSOMNIAC PRESS

Library and Archives Canada Cataloguing in Publication

Agnant, Marie-Célie
[Livre d'Emma.   English]

The book of Emma / Marie-Célie Agnant ; translated by Zilpha Ellis.

Translation of: Le livre d'Emma.

ISBN 1-897178-26-3

I. Ellis, Zilpha, 1938- II. Title.   III. Title: Livre d'Emma. English.

PS8551.G62L5813 2006   C843'.54   C2006-903792-2

The publisher gratefully acknowledges the support of the Canada Council, the Ontario Arts Council and the Department of Canadian Heritage through the Book Publishing Industry Development Program.

Le Livre d'Emma was originally published by Les Éditions du remue-ménage

Printed and bound in Canada

Insomniac Press, 192 Spadina Avenue, Suite 403
Toronto, Ontario, Canada, M5T 2C2
www.insomniacpress.com

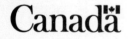

Dedication

This translation into English of Marie-Célie Agnant's *Le Livre d'Emma* is dedicated to the spirit of the two main characters of the novel and to the memory of the women whose heroic struggle against both the racism and sexism of slavery inspires their acts and words. These vestiges of colonialism in Haiti and the New World—colour bias and a lack of solidarity between men and women—are still alive because they have been internalized or accepted by many of their victims and because their brutal history and unspeakable atrocities are allowed to be forgotten and ignored.

Just as Flore, Emma's interpreter, advocate and benefactor in the novel, feels compelled to discover, understand and preserve her poignant message of resistance, so was I compelled to translate Marie-Célie's dramatic, revealing and enlightening work so that its message could be available to the large English-reading public. It is my profound belief that her poetic multi-level layering of history and personal relationships in this novel symbolizes the situation of many women in the Third World, as well as many in the multicultural and multiracial Other World to which they have emigrated.

It is my fervent hope that, through this translation, Marie-Célie's astute and perceptive evocation of some still unresolved consequences of slavery will now better defend the Emmas and inspire the Flores in all of us.

— Zilpha Ellis

Emma

I met Emma for the first time in the building facing the river. For a long time, the only words she could utter described the intense blue that permanently encircles a strip of abandoned land in the middle of the ocean, the place where her eyes had first opened on the world.

Dr. Ian MacLeod, who had requested my services as an interpreter, insisted on warning me: "It's complicated; the patient understands French very well: she expresses herself perfectly in that language."

He had spoken, I thought, in a slightly irritated tone.

"Then why does she need an interpreter?" I asked the doctor, without hiding my surprise.

He looked at me intensely, considering with the utmost care every word he wanted to use.

"Quite simply because she refuses to speak to us in a language other than her mother tongue. The help I need from you on this case goes beyond simply translating sentences. For almost two months I have been trying to formulate a diagnosis, or, rather, to unlock the mystery of her behaviour."

He turned his chair around and reached for a briefcase lying on a shelf. He took out a few pages that he perused with an expression of frustration.

"This is all I've been able to observe," he murmured, waving the pages in the air. "It's only about blueness: the blue of the sky, the blue of the sea, the blue of black people's skin, and about the madness which is supposed to have come over in the holds of the slave ships. This is all I've managed to glean from her long mono-logues," he added, handing me the pages. "A few words, caught in flight, like crumbs escaping from the beak of a fleeing bird. We won't get very far with this."

He had left his chair and was pacing back and forth in the room as he continued speaking.

"Because, of course, she sometimes forgets herself. She forgets her game plan and abruptly switches to French, a precise, even polished, French, actually. However, as soon as she realizes what she has done, she quickly clams up, and you can't get anything else out of her. At this point," he continued, thinking out loud, "it's probably important for me to be able to understand her adamant refusal to use French. I'm way off track, perhaps, but...I wonder if it might not be one of the keys to the mystery. All she does is talk, talk,

talk, without ever answering any of the questions I ask her. And what's worse is that she gets furious when I interrupt her to ask for the clarification of some detail. Two months of work," he repeated, rolling a pen between his delicate hands in an involuntary movement reflecting his impatience. His face, sprinkled with liver spots, looked up at me in search of an answer, an immediate answer, perhaps.

In his late fifties, Dr. MacLeod was a short, compact man with soft features. He was a courteous person, and, when he talked to people, it was in such a calm manner that his face took on the cold immobility of stone. But his slow gestures, his distant manner, hid a strong passion and an uncommon impetuosity in the practice of his profession.

"You realize," he said in a slightly trembling voice, his face somewhat strained, "my diagnosis will no doubt be decisive at the trial!"

The doctor stopped, stunned by the passion of his own words, which appeared to surprise him. Then, turning his piercing eyes on me, he assumed a tone which seemed calculated to suggest greater calm:

"I am relying on you, Flore. I have no alternative but to rely on you," he concluded, almost regretfully, before heading out into the corridor leading to the patients' rooms.

Along the corridor are two rows of doors that form large, white squares on the dull sea-green walls. This dreary green makes me feel light-headed, as though I've taken a sedative. I would have liked to have more time to try to understand, to reflect a bit, before meeting Emma. But Dr. MacLeod's impatience triumphs. I follow him. The tension in my stomach sounds like rumbling stones.

No more time to hesitate. With long strides, the doctor crosses the corridor, leaving in his wake the fresh fragrance of musk. In front of number 122, he stops, makes three sharp little knocks, then opens the door halfway and slips into the room. I enter behind him.

She is standing with her back to the window, her upper body leaning slightly forward, and she stares at both of us with the look of an stateless wanderer. Only Nature can explain the unusual excesses she indulged in when she created Emma. The results are astonishing: a disparate mixture of nobility and mute despair, of humility and arrogance. All that, imprisoned in a lanky body and a narrow face, a black face, with satiny, almost blue skin, a face as closed as a fist; on which her eyes are rolling like two runaway marbles.

In the silence of the room, Dr. MacLeod's voice seems to bump into the walls, into the metal posts of the bed, into the thick panes of the windows. The doctor explains, tries to demonstrate, with clarity and precision, the reason for my presence. His voice encounters Emma's closed face. Impassive at first, she listens without saying anything. Then, little by little, her look changes, and we read in it, Dr. MacLeod and I, a refusal that hardens. Suddenly, she beams the fire of her pupils at me, stares at me, sizes me up, observes me from head to foot, as an intense flush rises from my belly to my face. I open my mouth, and I feel, weighing heavily on me, all those words, coated with modesty, with fear and embarrassment, that I might have spoken. I open my mouth and no words come out. With her eyes, she quizzes me: "Why are you here? Do you really think what you are doing is useful?" she seems to ask me.

After a few moments, the doctor pulls up a chair, settles himself in it, and starts scribbling in a notebook. The scratching movement of the pen on the paper produces a strange sound, similar to the buzzing of a trapped insect. And it occurs to me that Emma's soul is imprisoned in the madness that has taken over her body.

Suddenly, she turns her back on us. She leans her narrow forehead against the window and aims her wild eyes out toward the trees on the grounds, then she looks back to the right toward the river that rolls its brownish water in the distance. Next, she comes toward us and goes over to an armchair into which she collapses, her body weary, as though she had just travelled a long distance.

"You brought in some reinforcement, Little Doctor?" she quips to the psychiatrist.

Her voice, a scream, even if it isn't loud. Her voice, a howl, although she isn't howling. A glaring light, the voice of a beggar, imploring, ordering, and pursuing you. This is how Emma's voice reaches me, already cutting sharply through my flesh, while her eyes are digging into me, burying her disarray. I am the interpreter, but suddenly I am mute. How can I translate Emma's voice and the look in her eyes? Dr. MacLeod understands. He puts an end to my torment as he stands up and announces:

"There now, Emma. Today, I only wanted to introduce you to Flore. We cannot make you use a language that you don't wish to use. Flore will be a part of our team; with her valuable collaboration, we will finally move forward."

We try to figure out how to say goodbye to her. Should we shake hands with her, smile? I don't know. I wanted to leave the room backwards, so as not to feel her wanderer's gaze on my back.

The door closes with a little muffled noise. In my head, Emma's voice buzzes like an insect imprisoned behind a window.

"As we agreed, Flore, our work sessions will be on Mondays, Wednesdays, and Thursdays," the doctor fires off in a staccato voice.

He presses the buttons in the elevator. I smile stupidly and extend my sweaty hand to him, repeating "Monday, Wednesday, Thursday," without being sure I will come back.

Outside the sky is bright blue, full of light. I walk as though I am pursuing a shadow; people bump into me and, like a drunk, I say "I'm sorry" without looking at them. I finally cross the street and go into a café to phone Dr. MacLeod. I'm used to working with him: some cases are very difficult, others less so. Most of the time, they concern women... Cases of depression caused by having been abandoned, by failure, and by dreams shattered on the frozen sidewalks of North America. But with Emma, I can't; I sense it: I won't be able to.

"Dr. MacLeod..."

Once again, the words don't come.

At the other end of the phone line, the doctor guesses what I am not saying.

"I've prepared a summary for you, Flore," he tells me rapidly. "I forgot to give it to you. It contains the police report on the murder, the contact information of the social worker who dealt with Emma for a short while. It would perhaps be good to have a chat with her. If you can pass by to pick up the envelope at the office before Wednesday, you'll have time to understand the case better."

Then he says goodbye, a bit rapidly again... an important meeting most likely.

I retrace my steps. The file is in the "out" box at the office. "Emma Bratte," written and underlined in red pencil. The secretary gives me the envelope with a smile she intends to be cordial.

"If you want my opinion on Emma, I don't have one. It's too complex, too weird. I don't have the keys to unlock it."

The social worker seems at a loss.

"All I know about her, I got from one of her friends, a certain Nickolas Zankoffi... I think that's his name. Maybe the last name is inaccurate, but all that is in the file. Go through it. The man was her lover. The child, Emma's child, was his. He's the one who told me. Some members of the hospital's Interdisciplinary Committee doubt that she did all those courses in Europe. I've never understood why. She was doing her Ph.D. In her house she had a crumpled little leather suitcase, filled with pages of that thesis she was always rewriting. I visited her several times. Her face was always haggard, her features drawn, her nails and eyes yellowed by cigarette smoke. She said she was working, and repeated over and over again that the colonialists of Bordeaux wouldn't destroy her!"

"Why Bordeaux?"

"I think it's at a university there that she defended her thesis, which they trampled on, as she says."

The social worker, also, seems to have too much work. She no longer handles Emma's file. The hospital has taken it over. It's better that way, since she doesn't have time. She can't give me any more information. "Emma's case is difficult, and the language problem," she says, just as irritated, "a red herring. What's more, it's a non-existent problem really, since Emma speaks very good French. And besides, how is it possible to show a link between her thesis and the murder of her child?"

From a drawer in her desk, she takes out an envelope containing a lot of newspaper clippings to show me.

"I've kept them all," she explains. "I had cut them all out to try to understand...something. Indeed, I don't know, I don't know why I kept them. But," she goes on with a pout of disappointment, "they didn't help me at all."

I go through the pieces of paper, which dirty my fingers. Emma was photographed from every angle. The hacks of all the tabloids revelled in her blue skin. One particular reporter, who didn't know the history or the geographical location of the island Emma comes from, described the town where she was born, a place called Grand-Lagon, in the Caribbean. "That spot," he wrote, "is as bad as the lepers' quarters in Calcutta." Emma's impoverished childhood made the headlines, and a photograph of little Lola was spread across the front page of all the dailies. The photo of her skinny body, in pieces, mutilated, ended up in everyone's garbage can among the dirty papers, the bits of rags, and the refuse carried away by the garbage men. Explaining the photograph, a caption, or rather, a cliché: "Black Woman Sacrifices Her Child...A Voodoo Act?"

Everyone could explain Emma.

Dr. MacLeod is right. Emma knows French very well. Hers is not the approximate knowledge of those who nod their heads when they recognize familiar sounds or words; she knows all the nuances, but, as she tells the doctor when he is preparing to leave her the following Wednesday, "a howling beast never borrows the voice of another animal."

It's my first time working in such circumstances: no more of the peaceful sessions during which I am able, without any particular effort, to keep the distance necessary to recover my complete and total liberty as soon as I leave the hospital. With Emma, I am translating not words but lives, stories. Hers, first of all. The suffering and madness of a human being's life are laid out plainly before me; Emma extends her arms to me and forcefully enters my mind and my whole being. Each of her sentences fills my breast with a dull pain, the same pain that permeates her body. I am also translating the history of an island, a scrap left over from the colonial period, a vestige of its cruelty, of its inhumanity. When my work session is done, I carry off with me big pieces of Emma's life. I carry off as well the furtive smiles that suddenly illuminate her long thin face and disappear in the blink of an eye.

Generally, Dr. MacLeod meets me in the little waiting room. The musk scents that precede him blend with the chlorine smell that is everywhere. I am right behind him when he enters Emma's room.

"Good morning, Emma," he always says as he opens the door, invariably in the same tone of voice, with the same little cough, as if to get his voice back or to gather up his thoughts.

Today, yet again, she is standing in front of the window, her eyes fixed on the river.

The first three sessions take place in an atmosphere of extreme tension; Emma doesn't answer the doctor's questions. She does not take her eyes off me as her fierce gaze darts out at me. At the same time she seems to want to gauge me, to make me lose my composure or confound me. For a face that is so long and so narrow, her eyes are much too big, but I sense that cowering deep behind her pupils is a portion of the answers to Dr. MacLeod's questions.

During the fourth session, Emma's tactics change radically. She has made special preparations to meet us. She is dressed with more care than normal; a lilac-coloured poplin blouse with its sleeves rolled up reveals her neck. She is seated, completely relaxed, her hands flat on her thighs, her feet resting on a footstool.

Dr. MacLeod does his best not to let his gestures give him away. Only his cough seems longer than usual, and he says simply:

"You seem to look better today."

Taking care to play her role perfectly, Emma pretends not to understand and gives me a questioning look. It's then that I come up against the exact meaning of my presence there in that room. I hear my voice. That voice, which is normally in control of itself, stammers, stutters, and translates in a whisper the words of the doctor.

I am no longer the person whose knowledge and sensitivity help others solve their communication problems, but rather the person who doesn't know, who no longer knows, her own place in the world. I balance myself on the edge of my chair, my muscles taut. Words come, not from my brain to my tongue, but from my gut. I am not simply an interpreter. Little by little, I abandon my role; I become a part of Emma; I embrace Emma's destiny. During that fourth session, it felt like my spirit left the room and went off drifting on the river along with Emma. It was then, I think, that I decided to follow her from beginning to end, to find Nickolas Zankoffi, to speak to him, and perhaps even to go one day to Grand-Lagon.

All That Blue

Emma contemplates the river as though she wants to complete a puzzle. Pieces of ice are floating on the surface of the water. She seems to have forgotten time; she has forgotten us, and she reels off words that my voice then repeats like an echo in the language of Dr. MacLeod. When I leave her that day, I realize that she has been doing nothing but describe, over and over, what she calls the blue of Grand-Lagon.

"It's an island within an island," she repeats, in a sort of incantation. "It wanders between the sky and the sea. You will never know how blue this blue can be, unbearable."

She shakes her head slowly.

"But all that is only appearance; I already told you that, Doctor. What is important is to know what is hiding behind the blue. I've spent a large part of my existence trying to discover that, attempting to understand. The first thing that you see when you are born into the world at Grand-Lagon is the blue. Some there say that the intensity of the blue causes a kind of madness... That's very likely, Doctor... The blue was there on the morning of my birth," she explains, her eyes half closed. "It filtered between my eyelids, and every other morning after that, I encountered it again. Since then, I have never ceased being shocked by what I see in the world. It's because of the blue, Doctor. It has always been all around Grand-Lagon, like despair. Basically, it's there to distract you from the continuity of the despair. In Grand-Lagon, you could say 'blue' like you were saying 'despair'."

Unpredictable, Emma leaves the window, takes several steps in our direction and starts to sing:

Kilima changu kidogo, my little hill
Kilima changu kidogo

Emma's voice rises, grating, while she approaches us and marks out a dance step in front of Dr. MacLeod. Caught unawares, I shrug my shoulders. The doctor answers me with the same gesture. I don't know what he jots down in his notebook, but I am surprised to find myself trying to memorize the words of the song: *Kilima changu kidogo*.

"It's a beautiful song, no?" asks Emma, in a more measured voice.

Has Dr. MacLeod noticed that after the song Emma seems to calm down? If I hadn't embraced Emma's destiny, perhaps I would alert him to it; I would point it out to him. In an intentionally complicit voice, I would say: "Don't you think that's a clue, a lead to follow up on?" If I hadn't embraced Emma's destiny...

But I don't say anything and, in order to assuage my conscience, I think: "It's like doctors who sometimes fall in love with their patients. That's what it is. I won't say anything to Dr. MacLeod. And if Emma needed to reveal facts that could harm her, I wouldn't tell him that either." Deep down, I am trembling like a leaf blown about by the wind. Deep down, I am happy to have chosen sides. Deep down, a voice whispers: "Sooner or later, one betrays oneself or someone else."

"Those who die in Grand-Lagon," continues Emma in her husky voice, "leave with their arms extended toward the horizon, in an ultimate effort to grab a piece of this blue that swaddles them all their lives like a shroud. They carry off with them in the back of their eyes the imprint of an inaccessible azure line, this blue of the sky that links up with the sea after passing over the mountains. It girds the town and slips into peoples' bodies. An indefinable melancholy floats in all this blue," she moans, lingering on her words. "It fills Grand-Lagon with a bittersweet emotion, a turmoil that I have never really been able to understand."

She half shuts her eyelids, as though exhausted by too great an effort, then with her jaw hard-ened, she murmurs again:

"All this blue and all its anguish are the only things alive in Grand-Lagon, where the living have only the appearance of being alive. I say 'the appearance' advisedly, because, on the boats, we were already dead."

She comes and sits opposite me now, her knees against mine. Her madwoman's stare par-alyzes me. I mustn't blink or say anything, and above all I must not change one comma of her words. I don't budge, and I do my best to resist the fire of her pupils. She must realize that the terror of the first days has almost disappeared from my face. I see the movement of her chest, which rises and falls; a vein pulsates near her temples. She leans toward me:

"You are here, repeating all my words for these whites, without missing a single one. Is it perhaps because you believe that they will see you for something other than what you are? That they will appreciate you a little more? Come on, you fool," she says to me, pinching up her lips with scorn. "You know nothing of the real story. From the way you look at this little doctor, the way your shoulders slump when you are around him, one can see. You must have learned everything from those books that they themselves have written to tell you your own history."

She laughs with a guttural sound that makes me shudder.

"I have also read some of those books where the history is truncated, lobotomized, excised, chewed on, ground up, then spat out in a formless spray," she goes on. "That's it, my poor Dollie; that's why they trampled on my thesis. So that they alone will continue to write for us, so that people will not know that already on the slave ships they stole both our bodies and our souls. You didn't read that in your big books, did you, Dollie?"

Pleased with her phrase, she repeats: "poor Dollie."

"That's what I'll call you from now on," she declares emphatically. "One could easily confuse you with a porcelain doll. You too must have played with those dull blonde dolls whose eyes open and close. All the little girls from home had them. We called them France dolls. Besides, it shouldn't bother you that I call you Dollie. I don't even have a name. In the old days, they gave us our masters' names. But nowadays, what's the use of that?"

She shrugs her shoulders, which are like two points, two peaks, under her sleeves.

"I hear the nurses speaking at the nursing station. Do you know what they call me? 'The negro lady in 122.' There is also the one in 124, the one in 145, the one in 136."

She goes again toward the window to contemplate the river while she continues:

"You probably believe that your straw-coloured hair and your eyes, yes, your eyes made to fool the night... because of that you believe they'll spare you? Alas, many think like you! And that's why the curse of our blood continues to hound us."

She closes her eyes and starts to howl:

"The curse of our blood! The curse of our blood, I tell you."

It isn't the first time she has screamed like that. I already know that no one will come. No one ever comes when she makes a racket. At night, they have to fill her with sleeping pills. It's because of these substances that she sometimes has a lost look. The corridors vibrate continuously from the screams of these women. Their howling reminds me of coyotes. But sometimes, they let out cat cries that make your hair stand on end.

"Here, one can scream without being bothered," she says, once she has calmed down. "Don't you want to scream with me, Dollie? You probably believe that you don't need to scream. You must think that to be a crazy black woman is the worst possible fate. Right? Just like them, I know; you think like them. Poor you! The operation was a complete success on you, Dollie. When one comes into the world like that, with those eyes of yours and that inside-out skin, and all those mixed-up features, one foolishly assumes that one will be spared the effects of their hate; one thinks that the mauling is for the others. And then one day, bam, one discovers that there are no two ways of being a black woman. Fifie was one of your kind, a black woman with that inside-out skin and all those mixed-up features. You'll see, when you learn my mother's story, Fifie's story, you'll see; it's useless to fight against one's black skin; it's like attempting to change the colour of the ocean."

With a penetrating eye, Dr. MacLeod observes his patient. Does he see that same glacial resignation that I discover in Emma's every look, in spite of all that talk which might suggest the contrary? Emma is sinking further into her madness; can she still be saved, is the question on the face of the doctor.

"You are here for this, aren't you, Dr. MacLeod? To listen to Fifie's story. She's the one who interests you, I know. She interests you because she is dead; I understand that. But you have to be patient. Before telling you about Fifie, I must tell you a few words about a time that is supposed to be in the past and that is called the old days."

She settles into her chair, as though for a speech, and continues:

"The old days, Dr. MacLeod. I mean to talk about the time of the slave ships and sugar cane; the traders were interested in lively black women. They traded us for firearms, for gunflints, knives, alcohol, metals. You see, we were worth a lot. All that was in my thesis. It took a lot of black women's sweat to fertilize the sugar cane, the cotton, the tobacco; it took a black woman's womb to carry the hands that would cut the cane and harvest the cotton; a black woman's vagina to drown the rage and violence of all the brutes, black or white. But today, the wood in this table is worth more than ten black women, isn't that the truth, Little Doctor? No one is interested in black women. That's why they are better off dead. That's why many of them are born already dead; right! Do you understand, Dollie?"

Upset, Emma stands up. She moves back and forth now, speaking sometimes to the doctor, sometimes to me. With a theatrical gesture, she seizes her chair and places it by the window. She turns her back to us and repeats:

"They are born already dead. They are born like dead tadpoles."

The doctor writes in his notebook. I would like to read his notes, to be able, like him, to take it all down, all of Emma. With her forehead against the window, she continues:

"It's our blood; I already told you. The blood that flows too heavy in our veins, this blood thickened by hate. Because, Little Doctor, everything started in a fight, a terrible fight and... hate won. But," she declaims in the style of a tragic actress, "I understand! It's because of our blood that the country itself is dead. It died from asphyxiation, and now it is rotting. And while it waits for a tomb, the scraps of rotten flesh that we are, the black men and women of this rotten country, we take our leave and take up the path of the ships. Do you remember, Dr. MacLeod, do you remember the first time, the first day that you came into this room, you asked me to 'recount for you the circumstances of my immigration'."

A little gurgling sigh escapes from her throat.

"Ah, it was almost funny, Doctor, you used such long words...sentences filled with flourishes."

She laughed heartily and tears glistened on the edge of her eyelids.

"'I don't remember anything,' I answered you. Now I know, and I can explain everything to you. If you still want to listen to me, of course."

The doctor looks at her, with a large question mark in his eyes.

"Yes," affirms Emma, who nods her head. "Write, Dr. MacLeod, write it down in your little notebook: 'Emma came to us from a colony of the living dead. A scrap of rotten flesh on the path of the ships, she was blown off course to this place. But it's just a stop; one day she will return to the path of the ships.' Of course," she continues, getting excited and making large gestures with her hands, "saying that all was dead is an overstatement, since there were hurricanes. Ha, ha, you've never seen a hurricane, Dollie? Your mommy, I am sure, must have hidden you in her skirts during the big winds. But Fifie never knew where I was during those times. She probably hoped that I would disappear, carried off by the big winds..."

Like a machine, I translate, my eyes locked onto the woman. I try to forget her, to forget her eyes, to keep alive only the echo of her voice.

"Ah, if you realized what it was like to see a hurricane come alive in a dead country. That force, that anger that wants to give life to things at any cost, but only manages to destroy them, uprooting and sweeping everything away. Hurricanes, you know, extinguish even the daylight. For whole days, they reign as masters."

She becomes gloomy, withdrawn, and murmurs:

"Only hurricanes manage to mess up the blue that surrounds Grand-Lagon. Immense noisy winds swirl; they tear off roofs, bend big trees as though they were reeds, transform their branches into enormous brooms that scratch the earth angrily. I will never forget, in the middle of the blue, the weight of the winds and the impact of their lunacy. There are the winds, there are the hurricanes, and there is the sea," she continues, "and as soon as the terrifying winds calm down, the sea decides to act up. And one can see the waves, like Amazons launched at high speeds, digging up the coasts, spitting out enormous spouts of foam, filling the houses with sea water."

She has stopped and, with her eyes half-closed, she now talks as though she were dreaming. Her voice, sometimes barely audible, becomes at other times a hoarse scream.

"There are the winds, the hurricanes, and the sea," she repeats, "but there is also that acrid smell of salt that permanently saturates the air, without ridding us of that breath of death, those mouldy odours of blood carried along by a wind of eternal madness from the sea, a wind brought in the holds of the slave ships. Did you know that everything came in those boats, Dollie? Silly question: who would have taught you that? It certainly isn't written in those upside-down books written by little white people. With their big words, they now claim to be studying the signs of madness in black women, while they refuse to understand what happened on the slave ships and on the plantations."

Dr. MacLeod, who had kept calm until then, bent over his notebook. He starts to nibble on his pencil. He realizes that I have stopped talking, since I am incapable of following Emma's rhythm and her disconcerting mixture of French and her mother tongue. "I am going to have to use a tape recorder to continue this work," I tell myself. I'll transcribe it afterward and give it all to the doctor. My thoughts are wandering when suddenly I see Emma swinging her hips as she approaches Dr. MacLeod. She plants herself in front of him.

"You're still sucking on your pencil, Little Doctor? You seem quite alarmed. What do you believe? After leaving the cane fields, black women learned to question things," she states slowly and clearly.

She leans over the notebook that he has on his knees:

"You're not writing any more? You can write this down too, you know, because it's the truth. Some of those black women even started to believe that they could act like men. They opened some big books. Ah, but they didn't just read those books; you should have seen them! They drank up the books; they swallowed them down whole! But, alas, books didn't change anything in their black women's lives. Useless harvest..."

She strikes her forehead with her fists.

"The result is that it's rotting in there. Who wants to know what is germinating in the brain of a black woman?"

She suddenly starts to sob, moaning like a baby. Her fists clenched, she rubs her eyes and sniffles:

"For us, it's rotting in there. Condemned, that's the word: we are condemned," she laments. "But we have dreams, Little Doctor," she blurts out, her eyes dry.

At these words, her face comes alive and she adopts a confidential tone:

"I dreamt once that our knowledge, our black women's knowledge, was changed into milk, into good frothy milk, into good, completely blue milk, so white it was, and we gave it to everyone to suckle. We were a colony of black women, and we moved forward, all in a row, bearing in our open arms our full breasts. Then some men suddenly appeared in immense ships; they captured us, tied us up, put us in shackles, and led us off. They sold us; they paid a good price for us, they felt us up, they weighed our breasts, the bids increased. Those who didn't want to think anymore threw themselves upon us. We were fountains of knowledge. Just as in the past they chained us up so that we would give our breasts full of life to all the little white children to protect the white breasts of their white mothers, we gave to all the milk of our knowledge."

With a quick gesture, she opens her blouse and exposes her breasts, whose areolas resemble two bulging eyes. Tottering, she leans over, brushing against the doctor. I feel dizzy, but I find the strength to get up to try to intervene. The doctor stops my movement with a gesture of his hand, while Emma straightens up and casts her gaze all about the room, her eyes reddened with fever, as her trembling hands button up her blouse. Then she collapses, shaking with violent sobs.

Dr. MacLeod gets up and glances at his watch.

"The session is finished for today," he comments in that neutral voice that he often assumes to remind people of the true professional that he is.

At those moments, not the least glimmer of turmoil, not the least spark of emotion crosses his face. Emma is probably right. For Dr. MacLeod, she is like the wood of the table, like the bed, just an object. I am starting to have doubts about the doctor's true motives. I would like to understand his method, his way of working. It is true that Emma never answers his questions, but I don't like his paternalistic, condescending tone when he talks to her. However, she does the same to him, I must admit.

"You don't want to know anything else, Little Doctor?" she intervenes once again.

"What a pity! I adore talking about hurricanes."

She looks the doctor up and down, arrogantly, and runs to put herself in front of the door, which she prevents him from opening.

"You don't want to leave; I haven't finished."

The doctor has already raised his hand to put it on the knob. He stops for a moment with his arm outstretched. He seems to be thinking. During this time, Emma continues her offensive:

"When you have taken all your notes, you will write a book, right? And no one will have the right to doubt your sources. They will be impeccable, no?"

She has a way of leaning her head to one side, and her body bends over like a vine.

"Another book," she goes on, "a book dismembering black women, and in which everything you write will be wrong. You will mix things up, you will change the figures, you will say whatever you want, you will be the expert, and you, Little Doctor, will be believed by everybody because your word is gold, even though you know nothing, absolutely nothing, of what is hidden under my skin."

Her tirade ends on one of those sighs which from time to time gurgle up from her abdomen; then, with slow steps, she distances herself from the door, crosses the room, comes tottering back to her chair, and sits down.

Without making a noise, Dr. MacLeod

leaves the room. I barely hear the click of the lock. I suppress my first urge, which is to follow him, to go away, to quickly leave this hospital room, never to return, to run away from Emma who is both crazy and too lucid. "It's all over," I tell myself, "my robotic work in the office of a doctor who is in a hurry to finish and who, more often than not, is bothered by my presence."

Dr. MacLeod is gone; I should leave as well. However, I stay there in the room, paralyzed, buried in Emma's tale. My mind no longer controls my lips. In spite of myself, I murmur and repeat her words, as though to engrave them in myself.

"Now, go away," she tells me suddenly, very angrily. "What are you waiting for? Do you think I trust you? Why should I think of you differently from all the others? Give me one reason, a single valid reason! You yourself don't know who you are!"

Panicked, I get up and gather up my things. She emits that gurgling sigh again and then quickly leaps over to the door, which she opens for me. She makes a gesture suggesting her disgust, and softly closes the door behind me. I leave the room with the intention of finding Dr. MacLeod to let him know that I'm quitting, that I won't be able to ...

The secretary doesn't raise her eyes from the keyboard on which her fingers are moving busily. She has recognized my voice perhaps.

"Dr. MacLeod? He has already left. You didn't see him? But wasn't he with you? Ah, okay.! I won't be able to reach him. You'll have to wait 'til Monday, sorry."

The buzzing of her machine follows me. Once again, I run away quickly and quietly.

During the whole weekend, Emma's words rob me of my sleep and my peace of mind. I come and go in the apartment; Emma's voice vibrates in my ears. Showers of hot flashes, sudden anxieties, come over me. Just a few weeks before, I had attended a seminar on the work of the interpreter. The expert seemed to attach a lot of importance to distance, to always keeping one's distance, the "appropriate" distance, he repeated over and over to us, as though all one had to do was install a barrier, some boundaries, and shrug one's shoulders once the work was done.

Time passes; I dream of space, but in front of me there is only an abyss, for nothing living or moving on earth is important anymore; the only thing that exists for me is a woman called Emma, and her madness.

Just as nothing can rid us of death, I can do nothing to avoid Emma. She is already a part of me. From now on, I must live her life. In a big notebook, I start to write about Emma; I rewrite the same things several times, but that isn't important either. Just like shells that catch the noise of the sea and stubbornly repeat its obsessive music, Emma's voice is ingrained in mine; she has taken possession of me, the way moss covers stones and the trunks of trees. In my writing, I speak to Emma: "I am writing to tell of all that burns in my body and in my blood and that I don't manage to convey to you during the sessions with Dr. MacLeod, so that your voice may live forever, you whose voice no one has ever listened to. I will write to your last drop of hate, and your voice, like a bell, will sound until the end of time."

As someone who has always handled the most abstract concepts quite easily, I suddenly feel like I am merely dispensing platitudes. I discover unexpectedly the sterility and vacuity of my words and, at the same time, how madness can be contagious.

Monday morning, early, I receive a call from Dr. MacLeod's secretary. She tells me that the normal session with Emma is cancelled, but the doctor wants me to be present at a meeting of the Interdisciplinary Committee. Full of apprehension, I ask myself about this well-known committee. What right do I have to participate in a meeting at which a decision will be made on Emma's fate? Won't this committee try to use me for its report to the court? For sure, they will want to know my opinion on what they call "Emma's strange illness". Dr. MacLeod always uses that word: strange. Does he suspect that I am wary, that I have packed away in the back of the closet, with my old school books, the sacrosanct neutrality that is the duty of the interpreter? Does he know that I have chosen sides?

I hear them already: "What is your interpretation of everything she is saying?" they will ask, even though they believe that I am hiding the truth from them. "And that way she has of expressing herself, that violence in her remarks. Can that be attributed to her culture? Could it be an atavism?"

I feel like I am caught in a trap, and I have to admit that I don't know the true answers, since I have never asked myself the true questions. Imagining that I have no questions, I settle for hearing myself say, rather often I must admit, that I have the perfect skin colour: just right, not too pale, not to dark. That is how they like us. "Like honey," some exclaim, "like a ray of sunlight, like a beautiful loaf of perfectly baked Belgian bread..." I used to welcome these words, sometimes with a stylish pout or a bit of annoyance, and I amused myself by scattering gold streaks in my hair to bring out the sparkle of my cat eyes, of my pupils "made to fool the night", as Emma described them.

"I don't understand what I am doing here," I comment to Dr. MacLeod as I enter the room.

"Don't be afraid, Flore," he says eagerly. "The Committee meeting is over. Everybody is very busy, so we had to start earlier. I submitted a report based on my observations of Emma. I concluded that we aren't making any progress. Emma has trapped me in the snare of her language, which seems disorganized but isn't at all, in fact," the doctor says. "We have to find a solution to this dilemma. We must change our method. Emma will not open up, I am sure, either to me or to any other medical professional. We have tried everything. In relations with shrinks, you know, it's a little bit like relations between lovers: you don't open up; you don't fully let down your guard, until you realize that the other party wants to give up any intention of being someone other than themselves. This is one of the basic principles of psychiatry.

"To come to the point, Flore, I am suggesting another way of working. From now on, it will be as if you were alone with her. I will be completely in the background; I won't intervene anymore. We will see each other before each session and I'll prepare a few questions in the hope that she will agree to answer them. However much she makes you a target, it's only a question of verbal attacks. Physically, you have nothing to worry about. The committee seems to find my proposal acceptable from an ethical point of view: it's in the meandering of her thoughts that we will find the key to her problem, since she refuses to answer the questions which are put to her directly, especially those which have to do with the murder of her daughter. Until now, she has neither admitted nor denied the act that she has been accused of."

"In that case, it's possible that someone else committed the murder, Dr. MacLeod."

"Come now, Flore," the doctor replies a bit curtly.

"But, one never knows. What sometimes can seem so evident to us..."

"Don't let's get off track," he goes on coldly, with that paternalistic manner that he can never dispense with, in spite of his amiability. "In fact," he continues, "neither you nor I are detectives. My goal is to understand what motivated Emma to kill her daughter, and you, you are supposed to help me to do this. By helping me, you will help her as well; that's the situation. The committee is of the opinion that she will eventually get used to your presence, and, little by little, you will get her to speak freely, clearly, and honestly."

Once again, Dr. MacLeod doesn't bother to wait for my answer. In the time that it has taken him to finish his proposal, I find myself in a waking dream, walking alone like an automaton in the corridors of the hospital. I have never heard of anything like that! At school, I hated my psychology courses. For me, Freud was the perfect example of a lunatic: he frightened me. But since I have been working as a professional interpreter, how many times have I been put in this same position of being a representative of a group "whose language and codes we don't understand." Of course, they always take the trouble to reassure me: "But Flore, you are nevertheless different." Emma was probably right in declaring that I was wrong to believe that they thought of me differently. After all, isn't this new strategy proof that I am nothing more than a mere tool in the hands of Dr. MacLeod and his committee? A tool that he wants to use in the cause of justice, of course. Does he plan to make me play the informer?

I try to read the doctor's thoughts. "She's one of yours," I think I hear him saying. "You will be able to understand what is wrong with her. We are willing to help her; we are doing our best, but we don't really understand your culture. It's up to you to discover what is wrong."

I could refuse the doctor's proposal. I don't understand clearly the reasons that compel me to accept it. The one thing influencing me, I think, is the idea that there is a veil covering the lives of black women, those with blue skin as well as those with "inside-out skin," as Emma describes me. Something tells me that by listening to Emma, I will be able to help tear away that veil.

As soon as I get home, I grab the phone book and find Nickolas Zankoffi's number without any difficulty. We arrange to meet.

A Legendary Love

The voice of Nickolas Zankoffi vibrates with an indescribable pleasure when he pronounces Emma's name.

"I could have loved her until the end of time," he says, "cured her with my love. But, since the beginning of her illness, when the police took her to the hospital after her arrest, she has refused to see me. I spent hours and hours begging the nurses to let me visit her just for a moment. Her orders were categorical. No visitors. I wrote to her; she returned all my letters. Something about her behaviour changed when she discovered that she was expecting that child and that she was already three months pregnant. The normal order of things, her movements, nothing was done in the same way anymore; she was no longer the same. A long time after she was committed, I discovered that she had tried to abort the baby. I found a bizarre variety of paraphernalia in a bathroom closet: a long tube with a suction cup at one end, long tongs, and an assortment of herbs that she had been steeping. Although I had been there, I had understood nothing."

As Nickolas Zankoffi talks, he twirls his spoon in his empty tea cup. For a long time, he keeps his eyes down. When he lifts his head, his lips tremble. It's then that I notice that his face is remarkably handsome, especially his eyes, which extend out to his temples. His skin reminds me of copper. He is tall and sad; his movements are slow.

It's hard to swallow my saliva. My eyelids flutter like excited butterflies as I look him over.

"Emma was crazy about history, especially the history of Africa. She went to Africa, to Senegal—she spent entire days wandering among the remains of Gorée—then to Benin, which she still calls the Kingdom of Abomey. She had assembled a large number of documents on the Amazons, the women warriors who, according to her, had defended the Kingdom against the European invaders and whom we have not heard of since. She never stopped asking me to tell her about my travels, about the lands I had visited, the women that I had loved. 'From what corner of the five continents have you come to me?' she used to ask me. And, each time, I would take up again for her the same magic tale:

My eyes, which slant toward my temples when I smile at you, were bequeathed to me by a Chinese ancestor. The Chinese were great travellers. My grandfather Liu married a Spanish woman, a hot-

blooded woman, as they say. My burnt-honey skin
colour comes to me from her, but also from Casamance,
from another ancestor: this one was a Peul lady. It's
thanks to her that the sound of the drum threads
through my veins like rum. Granada, the land that is
nourished by the blood of Lorca, gave me my mother.
She was one of the most beautiful women in the world.
I was born on an evening when one could harvest the
stars in bunches just by holding out one's hand. My
mother was a singer; she was travelling on the road
from Toledo to Granada when I decided that it was
time to see what the world was like, a world whose
movements had already reached me with such intensity
in her belly. The fairies entered a gypsy wagon. They
made a mark on my forehead with their wands and
baptized me "Vagabond of love."

I discover myself sitting there open-
mouthed, dazed, opposite this personage, himself half-crazy, who claims to have wished to
cure Emma of her madness. But I can't keep
myself from thinking that he's that man from
every continent that the world needs to cure it
of the chaos into which hate has plunged it. His
voice startles me as it gets suddenly louder and
takes on a sorrowful tone.

"Alas, we never know what tomorrow holds.
I loved Emma passionately, but I didn't take into
account that art of self-destruction which she
had inherited. Emma's refusal to bury her dead
meant her own destruction; she lived in their

shadow, a prey to their ghosts. During our discussions, she sometimes looked at me as though she wanted to see through my words, to the very heart of my thoughts, to hunt down the truth in me. However, she pushed me away. She constantly pushed me away; she couldn't believe the words of a man, she said. But I loved her so much that nothing had any meaning when she wasn't beside me.

"At the beginning, I had a terrible time getting her to relax. She was always in a hurry, in a mad rush: as soon as she got home, she tidied up, rearranged things, dusted. She cooked, ironed, mended, and didn't stop until she saw me get mad. Then she quickly took off her apron, put some cream on her hands, and came running. As soon as I had her in my arms; she would become restless:

'Do you want some herbal tea? I bought some fresh mint and verbena. I passed by the market.'

'I don't want anything but you, to be with you.'

'I have nothing to offer you; they stole everything I had,' she would respond, with an unshakable conviction.

'When one has lost everything, there is still love,' I would tell her.

"Since she had an answer for everything and no fear of contradicting herself, she would then object that she had lost absolutely nothing since she had never had anything...

"No embrace seemed complete enough or perfect enough to overcome the space that she put between us. Her violent harangues on the barbarity of the conquistadors were never-ending. 'Spain,' she would exclaim, 'should be charged for its refusal to end its slave trading until the dawn of the twentieth century. How shameful,' she would shout, 'what a disgrace!' One evening, in the middle of a meal, we were talking about rivers, waterways. She gave the example of the Amazon, I named the Guadalquivir. Her expression changed abruptly. I had no idea why. 'Tell me,' she started yelling, while she waved her fork topped with a slice of cucumber, 'tell me: have you ever thought about the number of Africans whose blood is blended with the waters of the Guadalquivir?' 'The Guadalquivir is just a river, Emma,' I responded obstinately. 'All rivers flow to the sea,' she triumphed.

"I tried in vain to defend myself, telling her that I had nothing to do with Spain. 'My veins contain the blood of all the continents, Emma,' I pleaded, 'and I am constantly called on to choose, to defend this place or that, at the risk of being excluded...' Her grimace would be full of scorn. And when she went out, whenever she went away, she would leave me in the company of the hate, of the monsters and phantoms brought over in the holds of what she called 'the big boats' and which peopled her existence.

"Do you think that she will get through this?" Nickolas asks me.

I can only shrug my shoulders, and he returns to his soliloquy:

"I have never been able to understand her. In the early years, I used to try to convince her that I truly loved her, since she associated my love with the sort of passion that is almost a perversion. 'That's what it is,' she would say, 'a collector's passion.'

"I loved her so much; I still love her. I feared losing her from the very first day I met her. It was in Bordeaux, in a little café, not far from the pier. It was late. She had drunk a little too much and talked to me about 'the dirty Bordeaux colonialists' who had 'trampled on' her thesis. It wasn't unusual to meet such foreign students, Africans or West Indians for the most part, who also were constantly denouncing the racism or discrimination that they had had to endure throughout their studies. That particular evening she was wearing a mauve turban that accentuated the smoothness of her face, which resembled the colour of well-aged purple-wood furniture. I had felt a red flush run up my neck when she beckoned to me with her hand as I passed by her table.

"I knew immediately that I was not dealing with an adventuress, but her mystery was impenetrable. She wasn't pretty, rather thin, a bit self-effacing. But she was more beautiful than anything. With her amaranth skin tone, she looked like an antique statuette. Deep in her eyes there shone from time to time sparks from an ancient sadness, which gave her a strangely soft look. Her gums were a purple colour. We became lovers. A few months later, Emma decided to follow me to Montreal. Bravely, she took up her studies again."

It is almost dark when I take my leave of Nickolas Zankoffi. It has started snowing. The streets are well lit, as though night hadn't come. Flakes glisten on the sidewalk and cling in compact balls to the juniper hedges, beaten down and stiffened by the cold. As I walk, I consider and reconsider the women that I know, and I discover with some anguish that they often spend a large part of their lives alone. Is it because, like Emma, the old pains have caused them to forget all the words for loving, for filling in the space between bodies? Perhaps, everything has changed much too fast for them. Love is probably no longer approached in the same way. Are they spending their lives waiting, like me and my sisters, for that exceptional being who will become for them a lover, an accomplice, and a friend? Why is it that their paths must never cross? Why must they be content with catching on the fly whatever happens to be handy in order to eat? Full of dread, I realize that women, even if they are still young, are more and more frequently living alone. To fool ourselves, we attribute this phenomenon to modernity. We talk about a lack of commitment, a fear of being tied down; at least that's what some of us maintain, who more or less accept our condition of being alone. For me, however, the question is a different one and has been asked more clearly recently: do men and women no longer speak the same language? One reaches the age of thirty, like me, so quickly, then forty and the despair which that age brings and which makes of us asexual beings that no one sees anymore.

My older sister, Gilliane, is not happy in this celibacy. I can still hear her, at dinner last Christmas, bitterly talking about male treachery. I remember our fiery discussions on the subject. "You'll see," she shrieked, "you won't be laughing the morning you look in the mirror and you think you see a raccoon, with large circles the size of a saucer around each eye, and that whole lump of flesh under the chin in need of some support... There are very few tricks to hide those ruins, Flore," she said bitterly. Gilliane's voice shook, pouring onto the male race all her accumulated resentment against the man who had left our mother and taken up with a white-skinned woman. "We are strong, it's true," shouted my sister, "can we be anything else? 'Strong and cold like marble,' the men must be saying to themselves... But, you can be sure, their women can read the suffering and desire under our shells. That is what makes them come running like mad cats when, per chance, their husbands dare approach us."

My Mom, during these moments, doesn't say anything. She simply goes to the kitchen, to do the dishes, to clean drawers that don't need to be cleaned, and to rearrange utensils, until the clinking of forks and knives replaces Gilliane's shrill screams.

As I think about my conversation with Nickolas Zankoffi, I'm suddenly torn by remorse. I rebuke myself: what right did I have to invade his personal life? It's true that he was only too happy to be able to talk about Emma, to pour a heart overloaded with torment into an empty attentive ear, to talk about those years of tempestuous and uncommon love with a woman who, as he said, was a solitary person, like a rock in the middle of a desert, like a wild bird.

I take my time going home on the icy side-walks. I am numb from the cold, stunned to see myself carrying the weight of my thirty years as though it were a heavy burden, to feel myself suddenly so old, and terribly alone. Since I've been working on Emma's case, a strange solitude is devouring me. Under the protective eyes of Dr. MacLeod, sitting in the corner of the room, I continue to see her, three mornings per week, to tape record her incoherent words, which I translate, transcribe, and submit to the doctor a few days later. Emma always ignores the questions that he takes the trouble to prepare. She only talks about what suits her. I don't know what Dr. MacLeod does with the texts I bring him or how he will use them in producing his analysis. Sometimes, I take out my copy of those pages, which I keep in a schoolbag, and I read them over and over, driven by a voracious curiosity, as though some revelation would be emerging from her words.

I walk for a long time to elude my weariness, in spite of the cold. The snow disguises the ice on the sidewalks. That makes me think about the dashed dreams described by Xiomara, another woman, this one from the Dominican Republic, for whom they called on me last month. With a chair she was swinging about, she had completely shattered the television set of the Block 3 Recreation Room in the Psychiatric Centre, as she screamed that she had had enough of being invisible. Totally naked, she had run through the corridors swinging her hips, shouting at the male personnel, asking them what she lacked in comparison to the *putas blancas*. "My three sisters had light skin," she screamed, "light like spring water. Me, I was the only *negrita*, the only one, the shame of my mother. Ah, if you knew how they scorned me! Do you think that this prevented their husbands from getting lost between my legs? I had them all!" She had to be given a strong dose of sedatives before they could get the chair away from her.

Nickolas Zankoffi offered to meet me again the following Friday. He has this crazy hope that I'll be successful in helping Emma. I can't explain what draws me to this man, but I sense that the whirlwind of madness that has engulfed him is also pulling on me, in spite of myself.

I am walking in circles in my room, unable to make myself leave, and I get to the café one hour late. He is still there, wearing his sad smile. He doesn't even wait for me to sit down before he starts to talk about Emma.

"I can tell you her whole life," he said, "her whole childhood, up to the time when she left Grand-Lagon. She talked incessantly. She was haunted by her mother, Fifie."

He remembers that before they left France, they spent a few days in Paris.

"Never had the flowers in the parks been so beautiful," he remembers. "It had rained frequently that summer. The rain would come, heavy, in large drops, a rain that thrashed about, fought with the wind, landed in torrents, in furious gusts. Like the mouth of a gourmand, the earth opened up, gluttonously swallowed the beneficial liquid. And, through all its pores, it sent back in puffs of fresh air, this incomparable gift that the sky had given it a few minutes earlier. The paths of the Luxembourg Gardens, which had been emptied for the duration of the storm, filled up again, as if by magic, with children, nannies, and strollers, attracted by the suddenly cooler air of that summer afternoon. Emma, though, seemed to be watching only the expressions of the passersby. She was sure that they must have been thinking that she was one of those women who was getting what she was owed for sex. 'I loved you from the first moment that I cast my eyes on you in the smoky bar near the pier,' I swore to her. I had the impression, from the very first day, of having known her forever, and of picking up a conversation with her that had been interrupted the day before."

To tell the truth, Nickolas has this special way of approaching people, like an animal, guided by his instinct, and, as an offering, he melts you with his sad smile and his ever present seductiveness. He sensed in Emma, from that first meeting, what others would have taken years to discover: she was genuine. He compares her to the sea: strong and serene, but just as unpredictable. The first time they made love, he recalled, it was as though they had been long-time lovers. They had met each other in a pile of clothes and had discovered—at least this was what he believed—that they were of the same race, the race of those who like the uncomplicated life and know instinctively the most age-old acts. Emma, a first love. Emma, the first woman. Emma, colour of the earth. Emma, real. Emma, a sea surge. Infinite clamour, she had filled his life.

Nickolas Zancoffi's sensuality, his passion, and his art of being larger than life bring me to believe that he may have frightened Emma. Perhaps this love, which was as deep as Emma's suffering, wasn't what she was looking for. Or did she simply believe that all that couldn't be meant for her?

The veil over Emma's life begins to lift the day she decides to tell us about Fifie, her mother. That day, in spite of Dr. MacLeod's presence, I feel so alone as I face Emma.

Fifie

"My name is Emma. You know it already, Dollie. Besides, I forgot, today I am not here to talk about myself but about Fifie. Fifie is my mother. We don't know any other name for her. The morning that my sisters and I free ourselves from Fifie's womb, that same bluish dawn stretches out over the mountains surrounding Grand-Lagon. We are five, five children all at once, five stillborn girls. What a struggle Fifie must have had to rip us out of her womb. I know nothing about that. All I know is the blueness."

At these words Emma's face tenses up and her body grows taut like a bow. Possessed by her narrative, very quickly she revives and goes on, with that lost look that often comes over her:

"The time and day of my birth aren't written anywhere, nor are they circled in red on some old calendar. At Grand-Lagon, calendars aren't intended to indicate years, months, and days. Aunt Grazie and Fifie line them up on the walls beside pictures of Jesus Christ with a bloodstained heart and women who look like Carnival queens. Decorated like this, the walls must seem less ugly to them. 'Only those whose houses have walls can cover them with calendars,' Aunt Grazie says, with those sibylline airs that she likes to put on. And she adds that it's right to make use of them to put some spots of colour on the walls; otherwise calendars would have no use!

"Before my sisters and I were born," Emma continues, "hurricanes, storms, and tidal waves served as time references for everything that happened in our country that seemed impor- tant. But later on, people no longer used these natural catastrophes and started situating events in time by indicating whether they had occurred before or after our birth. Our arrival in the world could have gone unnoticed but wombs and mothers, just like the number of children, are allotted in an anarchic and illogical way in Grand-Lagon.

"On our bit of island, our collective birth causes quite a commotion. The midwife puts all of us together on a large piece of cloth. She knots the ends to take us to the garbage dump or perhaps to a hole hollowed out between the roots of a tree. But at the moment that she is about to leave the room, I let out a piercing screech. In the pastures, the cows stop grazing, turn tail and run; the birds rush back to their nests. A furious tempest rages outside. Gray thunderstorms streak across the sky. The winds let out a sinister howl. No one remembers having seen such a violent hurricane.

"In those days, hurricanes all had beautiful women's names. They were called Flora, Hazel, Marilyn, Bertha. However, after I was born, no one could remember the name of the hurricane. According to Aunt Grazie, my screams covered the howling of all the winds put together. When the midwife realized that something was wriggling and yelling in the bunch of umbilical cords and twisted arms and legs that she had just pulled from between Fifie's bloody thighs, she stopped short, gasping. Then, digging here and there in the pile, pulling a leg from one side, from the other an arm that seemed to have been dipped in aniline, she discovered me. Yes, Dollie, I was here to stay, determined to know everything and to hang on for the whole ride.

"We looked like a heap of dead toads, Aunt Grazie always said, shivering in horror. 'That one,' she would say, referring to me of course, 'screamed for all the others whose voices we never heard. Poor Fifie, she was so afraid of her that I sometimes had to cover the mouth of that frightening thing that howled day and night.'

"In Fifie's room, opposite the bed on which she lies unconscious in a pool of a sticky blackish liquid, there is a large wardrobe of unpolished mahogany, with a plump belly like the paunch of an animal on the verge of dying. My scream, the power of my scream, makes cracks in the wood that spill onto the floor an army of startled termites. And, in spite of looking like a dead toad—that's how they described me—I already know all that, for I came into the world wearing five cauls on my soft skull: mine plus those of my four sisters. I benefit from the extraordinary good fortune of comprehending everything, of comprehending for five. In short, that's what scared Fifie the most. A child born with such a crown, that's unacceptable, but a tadpole that, in the womb of its mother, already appropriates what doesn't belong to it, that is guaranteed misfortune, the promise of hell for its next of kin, a tyrannical little animal, an evil, voracious beast, with eyes and hands over all its body. In the old days, such children were buried alive right away, the same day. But these days, things have changed, the crestfallen midwife seems to say, although like Fifie she would have preferred to see all five of us dead.

"I already knew that Fifie's hate for me was immeasurable. I swear, Dollie, I felt it as soon as I stuck my nose outside. Hate, you know, it's like a burnt or a rotten smell. It's not easy to hide it. So I learn in my very first days to develop survival reflexes—because I love Fifie with all my being. I am very much alive and I howl as much as I can. I don't intend to die. I hear everything they are saying, and one voice that I already start to detest compares my scream to the siren of a ship in distress. And I howl even louder, covering with my scream the annoyance and stammering of the astounded and panic-stricken neighbours who are wondering why. I would be happy to tell them that I am yelling so that they don't separate me from Fifie, so that I don't become mute. Alas, in spite of the strength of my desire, not a word crosses my lips; that is to say, no one understands the meaning of my screams. And do you know what, Dollie? Between then and now, nothing has changed."

Emma becomes more excited and raises her voice.

"Who understands the cry of a black woman? What is the word of a black woman worth, eh? You who've read all the great books written by the great men, what is the cursed word of a black woman worth? Who has ever heeded our cries?

"Aunt Grazie, Fifie's ever-present sister, is there, at the foot of the bed, on the day of my arrival in the world. With her arms dangling and her mouth wide open, she stares with alarmed eyes at that open orifice which has just expelled us, me and my sisters. With a silent prayer, she clasps her hands from time to time then wrings them convulsively. She grimaces and reels.

These sticky tadpoles that we are, my sisters and I, these bits of poorly assembled flesh, vomited by a swollen red gorgon, will make her lose her taste for living for many months.

"Fifie never talked about the day of my birth. It was as though it had never happened. Fifie was like that; she buried under her silence anything she didn't like. And I often think that I carry Fifie's silences deep inside me. Like stones at the bottom of a sack, they fill me up. Yes," Emma nods to convince herself, "just as Fifie carried us in her womb, I carry Fifie's silences in me. Without any words from her at all, I had to learn, from my earliest childhood, to decipher on her face the multiple truths linked to my arrival and my presence in this world. For example, listen up well: when Fifie least expected it, there would appear at the edge of her eyelids, at the corners of her lips, a pain that I alone would notice. It was linked, I know it, to my memory of the day that my scream, like a scalpel, had torn open her body. Like a draft of glacial air, it started in her eyes, followed a path down to her resentful mouth, then slid over to me, seized my face, my whole being. Fifie's eyes only skimmed over me but her pain penetrated me, tied me up, paralyzed me, and scorched me. In spite of everything, I told myself that this suffering, all the pain of this suffering, was better than being separated from Fifie.

"My first memories of childhood, besides my birth and the inaccessible blue, are of the dogs. The half-starved dogs with discoloured coats that we constantly chased away with stones, that fled, limping and howling with pain, but that continually came back, always came back, to hang around outside the shacks. I would take them in my arms, would bury my nose in their fur that was sparse and full of ticks. They licked my face and my dirty hands. As she always did, Aunt Grazie would start to stamp her feet and scream that I should have been born with four feet. Fifie would give me a look full of disgust, saying nothing, never saying a thing, never one word, as I rolled about with the dogs in the dust, letting out little cries of pleasure.

"During the year I turned four, I think, I started to repeat my dreams, so I wouldn't forget them. To repeat a dream, you simply close your eyes and follow in reverse order the path of the dream. There now, those are the words of real black women, you know, those who have never had anything but their dreams. When our people arrived on the plantations, they were stripped of their names, of their bodies, of their existence—don't make that face, Dollie, it's the pure truth I'm telling you. And for centuries, others used, abused, sold, bought, killed, rejected, ignored these human beings that we are, so what do you expect? Whatever you do, the only thing that is yours is your dreams. You look surprised, no? When you have finished your work with the little doctor, you will perhaps be on the path to becoming a true black woman, a standtall black woman. And to stay standing tall, you will have to be cunning, my Dollie, constantly cunning, and hang on to your dreams."

Emma leans toward me and whispers:

"Nothing provokes as much hate as a standtall black woman. They want to see all of us prostrate."

And as if to illustrate her words, she stands up and sticks out her chest before going on with her monologue:

"I wasn't yet four years old when I started to have this strange dream in which I am running in a big field; my arms are wide open; the wind is in my hair. With my head thrown back, I scream; and my voice rises up to the sky. The wind rushes into my ears, into my eyes; my mind is spinning. I run, and I hear the swishing of my brain, which is shaking every which way, then the earth opens up with a boom, but the falling rocks do not stifle my voice. In front of me, the trees are falling down, uprooted by the force of my shriek, their roots shocked, stripped bare, exposed. Nothing withstands my scream, except me. I remain upright.

"I wake up totally soaked, quivering in ecstasy. Voices are dwelling in me and they murmur in my ear that I exist, finally. Never have I felt it necessary to try to understand this dream. For the moment of the dream, I am happy. I am forcing the entire universe, and Fifie, to take my existence into account. I exist with a heart deep within me that is enraptured, overflowing with gratitude for this faithful old dream. Rapidly I close my eyes again to attempt to prolong the sensation of well-being that it gives me. But the feeling lasts only as long as all good things. I don't exist, not yet, in spite of the corrosive words of Aunt Grazie, who every day recites like a litany her story of the bloodied tadpoles.

"The moment during which I am trying to get back to the thread of my dream also serves as an escape, before I face the mirrors of the house, or the stares, alternating between shocked and irritated, giving my body a check-up, dissecting me, and measuring me. It's also the moment of the big decisions. If I can't change my physiognomy, I'll have to force the people around me, if not to love me, at least to take my personality into account, or else I'll have to disappear. Not existing any longer presents a dilemma, though, you know? I am part of that immense cohort of runts and tadpoles, whose existence is no more than appearance, but who paradoxically cling to it with the force of despair. And so, how can I disappear before pacifying, at least for an instant, that inextinguishable thirst for maternal love that is devouring me, making me itch, giving me no rest? If I die, I'll never have had the slightest idea of how the velvet of Fifie's hand might feel, the taste of her caress, of her kiss. How could I stop existing without knowing that tenderness, which I imagine to be like long shivers rippling down my body? Every day I go through all the steps I can take to try to satisfy this need. Not a night passes without my losing myself in the meanderings of incongruous dreams in which I succumb to the weight of Fifie's love.

"When I turn six, my experience in the practice of the art of surviving develops further, grows with amazing rapidity, and I also have this other dream in which Fifie takes to kissing me frenetically. Gluttonously, she covers my head, my neck, my hands, and my whole body with her kisses. Little by little, I am transformed. Like a chrysalis, with unparalled pleasure, I open up before her amazed eyes. My hair falls in streams of heavy, silky curls, and my skin, iridescent, adopts that golden honey colour that Fifie wears so proudly. I am a vanilla Popsicle. Over my face, my arms, Fifie runs her eager tongue; then she holds me to her breast and cries, swearing that she will always love me, her only daughter, her beloved daughter. I die of happiness as her arms lift me up to the sky, as though I were an offering. I take my leave, carried by the carillon of her voice that accompanies me, for a long distance, high above the clouds.

"'Yet another dream,' I think sadly, when I open my eyes. The reality is that I am considered ugly, capable of scaring away even a mole. And Fifie has never subscribed to the thesis that children are the wealth of the poor. She is incapable of the least gesture of affection, but I love her with an undying love, since that day when I had the unfortunate idea of 'attaching myself to the walls of her uterus with all the force of a demon.' This phrase comes from Aunt Grazie. That's what I heard her tell a neighbour.

'I assure you, Luce,' said Aunt Grazie, 'that Emma is not a normal child. She's a demon,' she yelped. 'Poor Fifie! She didn't deserve that.'

'It's strange, nevertheless,' commented the neighbour, over the fence separating our two houses: 'no one has the least idea of the real identity of the maniac who managed to do this dastardly deed to Fifie? Did she ever mention to you that she had seen an owl during her pregnancy? It's very possible, you know, Grazie.'

"Aunt Grazie shrugs her shoulders and sighs.

'You're probably right, Luce. But you've got to admit that fate and nature can have a way of being merciless!'

"I am crouched behind the parapet; Aunt Grazie doesn't see me. 'Hoo! Hoo!' I throw myself at her feet. She almost faints, hangs onto the railing, and then she starts to stamp her feet, waving her hands wildly, as though she had been attacked by a snake.

'You see for yourself, Luce,' she yells, her voice trembling with anger and emotion. 'You see how that owl behaves. Pour Fifie! I don't know how she will be able to live all her life with that thing.'

"Aunt Grazie makes as though she's going to hit me. Thunder growls and bares his teeth. She changes her mind.

"It's true; I haven't yet told you about Thunder," Emma exclaims as she opens her eyes wide. At those moments, her face becomes even thinner.

"Thunder is my father and my dog. I'll talk about him another time."

She goes over to the door, opens it and lets out a strident howl that resounds in the long corridor and curdles my blood.

"That's the way it is, Dollie," she says, turning back to me. "We are a few true black women in this wing. We greet each other this way from time to time. We scream for all those to whom they deny the right to be heard. Good-bye!" she interjects abruptly, extending her hand to me and pointing to the door.

After the sessions with Emma, I sometimes meet with Dr. MacLeod in his office, "to see what we have accomplished," he says. But all he does is pace the floor and scratch his head. From time to time, he stops and asks me how, in such a chaotic tale as this, Emma can follow the story line. How should he interpret the metaphors, the exaggerations, these images of unusual violence described by his patient?

I find myself at that moment thinking like Emma, in the same terms: "You won't get anything from me either, Little Doctor. Why should I trust you? It's not for me to give you ammunition. I've figured out your game. You pretend to want to help Emma, but you are working with the police. I will do nothing more than translate her words, believe me." Then, I announce to him my inability to enlighten him, even though for me these images are weaving the cloth of a universe upon which I am opening my eyes for the first time. A world where brutality has always been the law. Emma projects me into that opaque ocean of denied identity. With her, I've undertaken a long hard journey in the hold of a ship; in the hell of the plantations, I am suffocating; I'm a runaway slave, I have packs of starved dogs at my heels... I'm travelling along the banks of the Mississippi; I discover blacks hanged from the branches of sycamore trees. I see Billie Holiday, in agony, on the sidewalks of white America built with the sweat and blood of blacks, and her throbbing voice haunts my sleep... *strange fruit, strange fruit*, goes her song. Aren't we these strange fruits that survive thanks only to indifference? Silently I muse: "You won't get anything from me, Little Doctor. Do your job; I am doing mine."

Actually, I long ago lost sight of the basic purpose of my work. I rack my brain trying to find a thousand excuses for the act that Emma is accused of, and I tremble at the thought that, if they find her guilty, she will be sent to prison. My mother and my sisters are worried, are pressuring me to let the doctor know that I want to put an end to our collaboration. All I talk about is Emma, and I talk to them endlessly about the ways devised to avoid the suffering, the continuity of the suffering that is so evident in the existence of blue-skinned black women.

If I try to skip over certain words that, in my opinion, could prove Emma's guilt, I find myself making desperate efforts to help Dr. MacLeod understand her unhealthy obsession with ships, her continual references to the madness brought by the slave ships.

"Emma committed her crime shortly after her second attempt to defend her doctoral thesis on slavery, but, in my mind," the doctor objects, "that's only a coincidence. In my opinion, all was well planned in her head. The moment she chose corresponds with what in psychiatry we refer to as the 'acting out', the moment of putting a plan into action. That's that. Why this precise moment? Well, that is another question, Flore. In any case, it's better not to go into the details. I am sorry to disappoint you, but the cause and effect relationship simply is not evident."

He gets tangled up in his analysis, and he loses me.

"The panel rejected Emma's thesis because of a lack of coherence," he continues. "She was incapable of demonstrating certain facts that she was advancing. Can we use this rejection to explain her act?" argues Dr. MacLeod, without realizing that he is dealing with the very core of Emma's drama.

I realize that the doctor will never be able to find the keys that would let him unlock the evidence of the unconscious in his patient's narrative framework. The order of the events and her words are not the issue. Language remains the spanner in the works. We speak the same tongue, Dr. MacLeod and I, but we aren't using the same language. With Emma, I have learned to use other codes, I have discovered other clues. The doctor can't follow me.

"And if we were to discover that someone else committed this murder, Dr. MacLeod?" I say, looking him straight in the eye.

"You absolutely astound me," he repeats, as his face turns a very bright red.

Dr. MacLeod doesn't know that I myself am astounded by my daring and my madness. He doesn't understand that since meeting his patient, I no longer know what I am doing, or who I am.

Grazie and the Others

"During my whole childhood," Emma recounts, "my hatred for Aunt Grazie is equaled only by my boundless love for Fifie. They are twins, and, depending on the angle and the lighting from which they are observed, their features seem the same; they are the same size, and most people say that they can't tell them apart. But I can distinguish them by their bearing. Fifie looks like a queen. Just like her silence, her beauty is eternal. And Grazie, with her little shifty look, her skinny, faded face—they say I look like her," adds Emma who chuckles with immense pleasure, "has already buried any remains of subtlety and grace, which are a woman's best adornment. More than anything, it's their scent which differentiates them, their fragrance. Fifie's is mild and intoxicating; it lights me up and gets me excited, whereas what emanates from Aunt Grazie's skirts smells rancid, like wet rags, humid closets, and makes me nauseous. They never wanted to live far from each other. That's what Aunt Grazie claims.

But the truth is that Fifie has always been responsible for taking care of her twin who, in fact, only knows how to gossip, to hang around the yards and porches of the neighbours, waiting for the latest dirt. During my whole childhood, that's all I saw her do.

"My early childhood unfolds untamed at Grand-Lagon between Fifie and Grazie. I come and go, as free as the air, knowing neither the tethers of maternal love nor the constraints of friendship, for the children are also on their guard: 'Let's get away from her. She's the one who sucked up the souls of her sisters in her mother's womb. Look at her lips: suction cups. In one breath she can suck up all of a person's blood, drink up all of a tree's sap, empty a man of all his water. We mustn't talk to her!'

"But I know how to talk to the wind. I learned to decipher so many other languages, those of termites and land crabs, for example. Like them, I decided, from my very first steps on the sand dunes and in those mangroves that one finds far away behind the hills that surround Grand-Lagon, that I would always stand tall, even underground. The day that I made that decision, radiating with pride, I spoke about it to Thunder. He looked at me with his dog's eyes full of tenderness: 'what's the use of being a crab standing tall in a country that is prostrate?' he seemed to say. 'Yes, answer me that, of what use can that be?' Then, he lay down with his paw covering his muzzle.

"I also spent the first years of my childhood in all the nooks and crannies of the house, spying on the slender silhouette of Fifie, the most beautiful woman in Grand-Lagon. I have developed a way all my own of curling up in the darkest, narrowest corners, my knees up to my neck, my neck into my shoulders, my legs disappearing into my chest, my chest into my back, and my back into the wall. From there I am free to observe everything. Like a crab on the lookout, I scrutinize Fifie's lips in search of a word. I search out her gaze that always floats beyond me and her hands which continually shun me.

"Sometimes I take a chance. I crawl up to the chair where Fifie is sitting. I don't dare touch her, for fear that she may start to scream. I observe her, then before she looks away, I attack: 'It isn't true that Thunder is my father. Tell me where my father is!' And Fifie screams. She screams and stamps her feet, and I run away. I return to my position, my back against the wall. To my constant questions about the identity of my progenitor, Fifie replies with her cries and her screams or, during the lulls, the most obstinate silence.

"On the other hand, Aunt Grazie is never reluctant to recite all that she thinks she knows on the subject of my father. Like everything that is bad, he is alleged to have arrived by sea, vomited up by the ocean during a day of fury; it is Hell which, no longer able to tolerate his presence, has hurled him into the waves. Depending on Aunt Grazie's mood, or the seasons, the versions change. I had already heard her recount that my father was the only survivor of a country that no longer exists, a country punished by a terrible famine, during which the inhabitants and the dogs had been competing against each other, had fought each other for the same garbage, had torn each other apart, devoured each other, until no one was left but that man whose name nobody knew. Aunt Grazie had never seen him, but she claimed that he had the ability to make girls pregnant by threading his penis through keyholes. That's how she explained Fifie's pregnancy. According to her calculations, the pregnancy had lasted a good fifteen months.

"And again, according to Aunt Grazie, half of the paternities of the inhabitants of Grand-Lagon can without any hesitation be imputed to this nameless being. But this thinking derives from the days when the black men had been transformed into animals in the cane fields. At that time, under the eye of the colonizer, who was the master of the plantation, the foreman ordered them with his whip to service the women one after the other. In those days, black men were led to fornicate, just as beasts were led to water.

"My father was a very tall, bony man, with a long face, and cracked skin like the earth of Grand-Lagon, according to Aunt Grazie's description. He always wore a black frock coat, and a bowler that was also black and which covered his forehead. You could only see the whites of his eyes, she claimed, and, when he talked, his words were expelled through his nostrils rather than through his mouth, in a whistling noise that seemed to come from an animal that was both snake and jackal. 'That's what he was,' said Aunt Grazie, crossing herself and spraying the whole house with holy water.

"I listened to her in spite of myself, my body trembling with terror, all the while hoping that one day I would bump into this figure Aunt Grazie related that a woman called Élénie had bumped into him when she was returning from Bourg Salé. She had only been able to escape his grasp by warding him off with a large wooden cross that she always wore on her chest.

"Like a wound that one persists in scratching, I never stopped questioning Aunt Grazie and provoking her chattering.

'The dictionary is full of words for naming and describing fathers. Just choose one of those terms,' she advised me in the end.

"That's the day I decided to choose Thunder for my father. I was at least certain that he wasn't a ghost. He couldn't escape me, much less deny that he was my father, since he didn't talk. His love reassured me: he knew how to kiss me. Everything that Aunt Grazie said fired up my mind, gave me no peace. Then came the moment when I resented her terribly. I felt the hate invading me like a wave. Some evenings I saw myself in a dream dressed like a commander. With a whip, I would strike blindly out at a troop of lion ants and Spanish wasps. I would teach them to recognize that sweetish rancid smell which always precedes Aunt Grazie. I ordered them to assault her, to enter her through her nostrils, through her ears, and through her eyes. To my great joy, they would fill up her mouth, devouring her from inside. Aunt Grazie shouted, screamed with anger, and moved her arms like windmills. I watched her stone-faced, with eyes full of venom. Her body was becoming dotted with little holes dug by the ants; then she imploded, changed into dust that I swept up in an explosion of joy. Other times, I dreamt that I was holding her by her feet over the sea, forcing her to drink up all the water.

"I discovered later on that these tortures which I believed to be the invention of my disturbed child's soul were actually practiced back in what they call the old days. The women who refused the matings ordered by the commanders had to dig a big hole and pour cane syrup into it.

Then, they had to get into the hole and wait, wait for the ants to do their work," reports Emma, who exhales an immense sigh and represses a shiver that she manages nevertheless to convey to me.

A rapid glance in the direction of Dr. MacLeod reveals to me that his eyes are wide open from fear. In his white smock, he seems so slim, so pale; he looks like a ghost.

"The years pass, all converging. They are full of lots of tears and sobbing, vain prayers. Nothing seems to touch Fifie's heart. She never manages to forgive me for having clung so violently to her insides, my blue skin and I trying so hard to be loved. The years pass; Grand-Lagon remains the same, with its dry earth, its rains of sparse drops and its downpours, its hurricanes, its odour of death and its stench of blood which fill our lungs. Impassive, Grand-Lagon remains this cursed place of distress.

"One year, I am nine years old. The summer of that ninth year is interminable. In Grand-Lagon it starts at the end of April when not a single drop of rain has touched the ground for three months. In our desert town, the people are ill-tempered, anxious. They go about like animals, their teeth bared, for it isn't true that misery improves people. No, the misery of Grand-Lagon hardens their hearts. Blackjacks, pork rind, that's what the hearts of the inhabitants of Grand-Lagon are made of.

"It's in that same ninth year of my life that the men dressed in black arrived. Armed with guns, their faces concealed behind their balaclavas, they plow across the country. 'The prostrate country will never get back on its feet,' the old people predict, 'since, in order to nourish the kids, the women are learning to live on their backs, under the boots of the men in black.' I am delighted to be so scrawny, puny, with such dark skin. Behind their dark glasses, the men in black don't see me.

"That year I also come to know the vacuum effect: that sensation of glacial cold which grips my insides, when I discover in the pupils of my comrades that almost sensual joy that they feel at making me suffer when I get close to them and, brusquely they move away, disperse in little groups while making piercing screams. A bigger and bigger distrust surrounds me at school, coming from all the homes where they proclaim that so much disgrace and intelligence united under the same roof are surely the work of some devil. 'Do you see her lips? Like the snout of a warthog! And what about her expression, like that of a madwoman who sees her image in a mirror for the first time? Jesus, Mary'...

"The children have learned to make the sign of the cross when my eyes encounter theirs. At school, no one plays with me. I'm used to hearing: 'Above all, stay away from her. She's worse than twins and children born with twelve fingers. We've never heard of this in Grand-Lagon, or even in the whole country, five children vomited at once! We're warning you! Don't even sit in front of her; with that way she has of looking at you from below, she is very capable of infiltrating your soul!'

"At recess, I join up with Thunder, who has been waiting for me under the flamboyant tree. I tell him that the teacher ignores me. She never looks at me, never thinks about asking me questions. It doesn't matter; I'm the most intelligent in the class. I know it because I understand everything even before her explanations. So I no longer raise my hand during quizzes. All I do is listen to the others mumbling their answers. In the evening, they tell their parents that the tadpole has the power to suck up all their brain marrow. Because of that, they can't retain anything that the teacher tells them. The teacher has a high-pitched voice, a voice of tires that screech on rusted metal. When she speaks, I get the urge to let out a loud scream to make the walls of the classroom collapse. The classroom walls are covered with leprosy. There are not enough calendars to hide the holes on the walls. The walls are like a sponge. When it rains, they soak up the water and we can detach big pieces from them to make into mud cakes that we throw and that stick to the black board like large buboes.

"The teacher has a voice that makes you want to strangle her so that she'll be quiet. As with Aunt Grazie, I would imagine myself holding her over the ocean to force her to drink all its water. When I am tired of listening to her voice and to the others who are mumbling the lesson, I put my head down on my desk; I fall asleep and I dream. When the clock announces the end of classes, I wake up. Flows of drool drip onto the desk, onto my exercise books; I don't care. In my dream, I find my treasure and a happy Fifie smiles at me. When I wake up, the pupils snigger quietly, hiding behind their workbooks, and the teacher, her eyes full of dread, turns her head away when her eyes meet mine. What does the teacher matter, her fears and her chatter? I go back to Thunder and we roll around on the ground for several minutes. Then I go home to see Fifie, even from afar, with the hope of managing to brush against her, to breathe in the smell of her skin, to look at her clean hands and pink nails with glints of purple, and to imagine for a moment that they are caressing me. I need nothing but the love of Fifie, and of Thunder, my father.

"Everyone claims that I look like a badly assembled puzzle. When I was very tiny, my arms hung on each side, as though they had been attached to my body after my birth by some bone-setter. My head was enormous, covered with scattered peppercorns, and my skin, so very black, was sometimes shiny and looked almost blue. I have already told you that it's above all because of my skin that they hated me. All the same, no matter how much I turned around and around in front of the mirror, asking myself what should be changed, nothing ever occurred to me. It's true that my hair is very rough, and my skin the colour of coal; but I don't see their link with all those words lined up in the dictionary under the word 'black': 'disastrous', 'doleful', 'dreadful', 'hateful', 'marked by evil', 'nasty'...

"Each day I empty my heart, I bury everything that could weigh it down; I even try to get rid of my desire for some maternal tenderness, so that only the emptiness is left. Emptiness like darkness, immense, emptiness like the blue, immensely empty. Little by little, I get a taste for this emptiness which gives me a delicious dizziness. A sensual joy, an extraordinary enjoyment seizes this empty heart, and that has no name.

"That summer of my ninth year, the month of May explodes the hibiscus flowers before their maturity. Open wounds, they hang lamentably on their branches. The mangoes open up as well because they have ripened too rapidly;

they ripen before their time. Like slashed teats, they let drip their viscous drool and fill the air with a sickly sweet odour like Aunt Grazie's; it mixes with the bitter odour of the dust, turns one's stomach, and spreads madness in the ranks of the flies and bees. School closes at noon. It's too hot. The madness that lurks everywhere enters the schoolyard at a full gallop. I go home with Thunder on my heels. I have already told you about Thunder. I brought him home from the garbage dump. The day I met him, he was full of holes, covered with bites. His skin, in places, was hanging off of him. I could see his bones; they were white, like fragments of gypsum in the middle of flesh. He had probably routed an army of starved dogs. I helped him to get better. Since then he hasn't left me and he sleeps with me. At home he is always beside me. As soon as I lift my foot, he lifts his paw and follows me. When I go to school, he comes with me and waits for me, lying under the flamboyant tree at the entrance near the gate. We are equally ugly, people say, both of us scruffy and ill-tempered. Aunt Grazie, however, goes even further. Thunder and I are identical, she maintains.

'That's normal, since he's my father,' I answer. 'He's the only one who kisses me, and he cries and consoles me when I hurt.'

"It's that same year that Thunder officially becomes my father. At the beginning, it was a question of a secret that we shared, he and I. To make things official, I forged a birth certificate that I carry around everywhere with me. In place of *Father: Unknown,* I wrote, *Father: Thunder Brisebois.* I held his right paw and slid a pen between his toes. We drew the letters. I call him Daddy Thunder.

"That summer, Thunder and I go together all over Grand-Lagon and the surrounding countryside in search of the treasure that will win me the affection of Fifie. Everywhere I go, there is nothing but desert, the smell of rotten mangoes, the buzzing of flies, and the blue... All the blue that comes from the sky dives into the sea, embraces the mountains, encircles the city. All this blue for nothing. I close my eyes and I see my indigo lungs. All this blue for nothing... cold, like the scorn in the corners of Fifie's lips.

"It's that summer of my ninth year that I make the firm decision to successfully seduce Fifie before the end of the summer vacation by putting my hands on the most precious treasure that exists in Grand-Lagon. Early in the morning, I disappear with Thunder, persuaded that I will bring back this treasure that is hidden somewhere and that I only have to find. It's not possible, I tell myself, that life holds nothing more for me than this blue which never changes nor ages, than those weird dreams, than Fifie's indifference or scorn and that hatred which constantly splatters me. No matter how much I try to console myself by telling myself that I have Thunder, my thirst for some maternal love continues to multiply tenfold. Without Fifie, I am nothing. I repeat to myself: nothing whatsoever, nothing at all. Brutally the wind brings back the echo of my voice: nothing, nothing whatsoever, nothing at all. I search in the bushes and cross river beds, I climb the hills and pick wild orchids that I dream of presenting to Fifie but I trample them underfoot before getting home. Tirelessly, I dig up to my shoulders into the mountains of refuse haunted by the dogs, by people poorer than us, and by the rats. I go into the neighbours' yards, dodge in and out of attics from which people chase me away with blows from leather straps, while they scream and make the sign of the cross.

"Once, I find myself in a cave inhabited by monsters and horrible creatures, sure that there I will encounter the coveted object, that dream object which will put an end to the scorn that Fifie and Aunt Grazie are crushing me with. Water is seeping through the ground and the walls, which are covered with little insects of all kinds and all colours. That day, Thunder and I sow destruction in the ranks of the bats. Panic-stricken, the pipistrelles brush by us with their ears tapered like knife points and bump into the humid boulders with a dull noise. Armies of scorpions and centipedes, wriggling like worms, flee in every direction to take cover under the rocks.

"Thunder and I have already waged so many wars. We know how to rout the most formidable enemies. Evening surprises us in that cave, in the process of unearthing an old tin box filled with cartridges. After spending a moment gazing at it, then taking inventory, we decide to put it back, unconvinced of the usefulness of such a find. I could use the cartridges to make holes in the body of Aunt Grazie, but I would need a gun. Only the men in black have guns. So I bury the box again, deeper. I undertake to enlarge the hole with a piece of metal. If I am unable to find a gun, I tell myself, I would be able to use the gunpowder to make a poison that I would administer to Aunt Grazie. I am digging zealously, and I see parading in front of my eyes the impressive list of deadly ingredients for preparing this poison which, just like acid, would corrode her guts. I think first of all about the contents of that demijohn, hidden in a sideboard in her room, which she says is holy water from Rome and which she spends her time sprinkling around the house. Some urine from Thunder and, of course, from me, would be necessary, and something more: scorpions and centipedes reduced to a purée, with some little Madeleine snakes. Some lime; I won't have any trouble finding some, it's everywhere. That's what people use to whitewash their houses in Grand-Lagon. Wood ashes, dried toads, they aren't lacking either: the sun roasts them even before they leave their ponds. Of course, I would also go to the cemetery. It overflows, they say, with ingredients used by witches. They go there at night to get their supplies.

"Digging up the earth of the cave that is both stone and clay proves to be a difficult task, so I have lots of time to prepare the poison in my head. Eventually, I bury the cartridges, and suddenly I perceive the face of Aunt Grazie springing up in front of me. In the cave, the pipistrelles panic in every direction and make shrill little cries, but I don't let myself get distracted. I have pointed a pistol at Aunt Grazie's temple. Under Thunder's threatening gaze, I hold a jug out to her. With her eyes rolled back, her thick tongue, her face smeared with the blackish slimy liquid, she drinks, making all sorts of disgusting noises. The grotto fills up with a strong sulfur smell. Aunt Grazie collapses at my feet, and her face, which has doubled in volume, goes from mauve to blue then to purple, with big green and black blotches. Suddenly, her body becomes liquid; her eyes, white and enormous, float in a black slimy pond, which disappears in big bubbles into the humid floor of the cave."

With muffled steps, Dr. MacLeod approaches the door, indicating to me that he will be back in a few minutes.

"You won't leave, Dollie," Emma interjects, interrupting her narrative. "I am tired, it's true, but I still have lots to tell you. You can't leave," she tosses out again in a plaintive tone that contrasts with the vigour of the story that she takes up again without delay.

"Another time, Thunder and I found some bones. They seemed to be those of a child. A few days earlier, the sea had risen to the level of the city and had invaded everything, even the houses. The people had had to find refuge, some on their roofs, some in the trees. Aunt Grazie and Fifie had done the same as the others; they had taken refuge in a flamboyant tree and had left me in the house, in the hope that the sea would carry me off with it. But I had piled the chairs one on top of the other on the table; then I had perched myself at the very top, near the roof. My head was bumping against the joists and I had shoved my knees up to my chin, my legs into my chest, my chest into my back. After three days, the sea withdrew. It withdrew, leaving all sorts of strange things: fish skeletons, empty shells, bones... When after these three days Aunt Grazie and Fifie came back, they seemed so vexed to see me there, in the flesh, such distress was written on their faces and in their smallest gestures that I thought I had better leave.

"I hung around a long time on the shore. When I entered the cave with Thunder, there was a strong smell of humidity and rot. It's Thunder who made the discovery. He started to scratch the ground furiously, moaning all the while. Suddenly I saw a little limb appear, an arm I think. Someone must have buried an unwanted child there. I imagined a woman, her thighs open wide, her vagina in a death howl, her panicked hands on her belly. I sensed her screams and I felt awful.

"After having passed a good hour asking myself if the woman had come in the night all alone to force the baby out of her belly and then to bury it, I started to harass Thunder with my questions.

'Do you think that she buried it while it was still screaming? Was it a girl or a boy? Didn't she have to stick clumps of earth in its mouth to keep it quiet? Did it have skin that was too blue, her child, bluer than mine? Is that possible? You don't know?'

"Thunder doesn't answer a thing. He just looks at me with his dog's eyes and his wet tongue that hangs to the side. At that moment I feel an irresistible urge to cry. I close my eyes very hard and I clench my fists; then I start to scream, like in my dream, as though I was waiting to see the earth open up and the mountains crash down on me. After a while, I gather up the bones in my dirty handkerchief and I go off to bury the bundle at the foot of a flamboyant tree, with a fistful of blood red petals.

"My peregrinations with Thunder always lead me to new discoveries. That encourages me to continue my search. The day isn't far away when I will get the treasure. I'm certain of it. I only have to close my eyes to delight in the vision of Fifie opening her arms to press me to her heart when I give it to her.

"Another time, it's in the cemetery. It's still daylight. I don't dare go there at night like the witches do. All around the cemetery there is a tall paling fence that I try to climb, without success. Wood splinters, the length of needles, pierce my hands. Inside that, they have erected a cement wall, with a line of glass shards at the top. The cemetery, a real fortress. That doesn't discourage the thieves, since they steal even from the dead. It's Aunt Grazie, the one who sticks her nose into everything, who makes that claim. She tells how the Duplan family had gone back to the cemetery the day after the burial of Mr. Duplan and apparently found him sitting on his grave as naked as the day he was born. His casket had been taken, to be sold back to the undertaker, and it seems that his clothes had been seen in one of those department stores that belongs to the big shots in the capital. Mrs. Duplan had a sudden heart attack, and has been unable to utter a word since then.

"On the day in question, I am trying to get into the cemetery, when, through a hole in the fence, I glimpse a rat as big as a puppy. I am sure it must feed on the corpses, like Mr. Duplan's, that thieves exhume to steal their clothes and don't bother to rebury. I am there contemplating all these things when I see the rat arch its back against the wall and take its teat in its claws to give to a baby rat that grabs onto it. The little one drinks gluttonously while squealing and moaning. And without knowing why, I suddenly feel sad, and I am envious of the baby rat and its little moans of pleasure. It's definitely that evening, on returning home, that I start to tell that story, to tell it out loud to myself, with the hope that Fifie and Aunt Grazie will hear me. Aunt Grazie hears everything, since that's her line of work. But that evening, she pretends the contrary. So I shout, asking Fifie if she nursed me when I was a baby. I remembered all that when I decided to nurse Lola. Yes, that scene came back to me as if..." Emma closes her eyes a short moment and frowns, "as though it had happened yesterday. I would see Aunt Grazie again, with her sly face. In fact, it's not true that I look like her."

Abruptly, Emma asks me:

"You don't have any children, Dollie?"

Paralyzed with surprise, I don't know what to answer. My back stiff, my mouth closed, I shake my head. She looks at me intently and says:

"Do you know you can produce a child as black as the night? You know that, eh, Dollie?"

I nod my head. She gets up and goes toward the window, murmuring:

"When the weather is very good, I think about Lola. She was beautiful."

In spite of myself, I hear myself asking her:

"Who did Lola look like?"

She looks at me again, looks at me for a long time, then she says:

"Lola, she looked like the wind."

She says that before withdrawing into herself. Her shoulders hunched, her back bent over, she becomes silent. It's the first time that Emma has spoken of her daughter, and I feel like I have been caught off guard. And that is not the last surprise, for suddenly, her voice resonates again.

"When I asked my question, about the baby rat, Aunt Grazie opened her eyes, horrified. Her mouth made that horrible noise of hissing water that simultaneously expresses scorn, disgust, and rage, while Fifie went into a magnificent trance. Her face changed colour. With her eyes and her fists closed, she screamed, stamped her feet, and breathed heavily, as though she lacked air; then she fled, still screaming."

An indecipherable smile floats on Emma's lips when she mentions Fifie's trance. She continues with an ironic look on her face:

"On school holidays, I go off to look for my treasure and return home only when the Angelus sounds. I come back, looking preoccupied, my mouth enlarged by a circle of white powder, my lips dried up from thirst and fatigue. My face is covered with scratches, my hands are full of thorns, and the hope of acquiring that treasure is no more than a ball of phlegm that moves up and down between my belly and my throat.

"When I arrive, I am invariably welcomed by Aunt Grazie's shouting and Fifie's obstinate silence. Aunt Grazie says that they are worried about me wandering until nightfall in that hostile area and climbing those steep mountains. 'You are going to tumble to the bottom of those cliffs,' predicts Fifie one day in spite of herself. Her voice breaks when she announces her prophecy, as though she truly feared for my life. For the space of a moment, a spark of hope lights up in me; a shiver shoots through me: 'She probably loves me a little,' I tell myself, 'since she fears for my life!' If I tell her there are so many times that I have almost found myself at the bottom of these cliffs, or that I fell not long ago and that Thunder saved my life, would she perhaps throw her arms around me to kiss me, to hug me in her arms?

"Furtive, ridiculous hope. 'That won't work,' I tell myself, after discovering a sharp glint of suffering in her expression. So, I lower my head and leave to curl up in a corner. I finally understand that Fifie trembles from despair when I arrive, at seeing the evening bring me back alive, and that, with all her heart, she hopes that one day I will end up at the bottom of the cliffs. Before I was born, she must have tried everything to get rid of me: baths of smelly leaves, macerations of bark, long needles, metal hooks, bamboo stalks. Invincible, I clung onto her womb with my lips, those two suction cups that she can't stand.

"Sometimes Fifie starts to cry. She never makes any noise when she cries. The movement of her chest rising and falling, and the irrepressible trembling of her shoulders are the signs that she is shedding tears. Aunt Grazie consoles her: 'You have to go all the way, Fifie,' she says, mopping her face and kissing her... 'all the way.'

"From hearing these words from my aunt, I end up adopting them. When I leave to search for my treasure, with Thunder at my heels, while hurtling down the hills, clinging onto the undergrowth, climbing the sheer rocks, I murmur: 'all the way Emma... You have to go all the way.'

"Fifie never takes part in my conflicts with Aunt Grazie. She pretends she is not involved. She adopts the same attitude when I talk about Thunder. She has never denied that Thunder is my father. Fifie is a sphinx. Only her sighs let you detect any kind of human nature in her. When I fight with Aunt Grazie, using nasty remarks, Fifie seems to say by her silence that it's only a vulgar question of dogs.

On the edge of the river, I fell asleep
Dreaming of the earth and of paradise
I lay down in the grass
To listen to the wind
To listen to the singing of the grass in the fields

"I started announcing my evening arrival by singing. My voice is very melodious. Nonetheless, my singing always seems to upset Fifie and Aunt Grazie. I sing anyhow, to avoid the 'ohs' of surprise mixed with fright that they can't repress when I appear.

"The years roll on. This particular year, I'm eleven years old. One morning, Fifie wakes me up at the moment when I'm dreaming that she is holding me in her arms and covering me with kisses. I pull myself away from that vision, wearing what I believe to be my most beautiful smile. I offer it to her as I extend my arms. As

fast as lightning, Fifie turns her head away. I
have only enough time to glimpse a spark of flint
in her pupils. It tears up my soul. I remain pet-
rified in my bed, with my feet frozen and thousands of glass shards in my throat and my chest.
My skin is full of slivers. In Fifie's throat, her
voice chokes as she enjoins me to get up and go
with her to Dead End Plain, to Smelly Springs.
It's one of the rare times that she speaks to me.
So, without balking, I do what she orders. I get
up and dress myself, put on my rubber sandals
and follow her.

"Smelly Springs, Azwélia... my blood is no
longer flowing in my veins. An irresistible urge
to flee torments me, even though for the first
time I am so close to Fifie, alone with her. She
has even ordered Aunt Grazie and Thunder not
to follow us. We get into an empty bus which
goes huffing and puffing up the hills that surround Grand-Lagon. After a few miles, the
driver decides that there are not enough pas-
sengers to go as far as the Springs. His vehicle
rumbles, backfires, creaks, and smokes all at
once. He stops. We get off without flinching,
and we cover three quarters of the way on foot.
It is early, but the sun is already high in the sky;
on my skull, it explodes like a hail of bullets.
The peppercorns of my hair are roasting. It
even seems to me that I can smell its insistent,
spicy odour that harasses me, penetrates my

nostrils. Sweat forms thousands of little streams that inundate my face; my eyes are cooking in this burning liquid which drips from my forehead and threads its way under my eyelids. My blouse is soaked. In a short time my handkerchief is transformed into a grayish ball, inadequate to the task. I mechanically thrust my steps into the dry earth, in Fifie's footprints, taking care to keep far away, deep down inside of me, my sighs of exhaustion, to repress my urge to break out into sobs and especially my tenacious urge to start screaming, like in my dream, so that the earth may open up, so that the mountains come down upon us in a furious rockslide and bury us, Fifie and me.

"With her light step, Fifie takes the lead with big strides. She is so agile; she looks like she is flying. Her steps barely touch the ground. A violent desire comes over me to touch her dress, a light fabric like her step, like gauze, immaculate white, so bright in the white light of the morning, it hurts the eyes. I advance my hands. But I don't dare. I am afraid that she might start to scream.

"Fifie's dress flutters. Her skirt ends in points; it swells up from the thrust of the wind. The fragrances of cinnamon and clove, that perfume which emanates from the oil she uses to give shine to her hair, reaches me. Fifie is beautiful, one of those beauties without fluff and without artifice. A complete, autonomous beauty. Fifie doesn't need anything to be beautiful, especially not from me; still less does she need my love. She has delicate little hands with brilliant nails, finely edged ears and lips. She is beautiful like a stone, polished by the sea: hard, strong.

"My eyes are sometimes riveted on the ground, observing the comings and goings of the insects between the cracks, sometimes riveted on Fifie's back, on her tiny waist. And I say to myself: Fifie is an asphodel, a mute and beautiful flower, and I don't exist. As we get closer to the Springs, in vain I beg her to turn back. She doesn't unbutton her lips.

"During those three days at Azwelia's, in the course of those strange ceremonies in which I took part in spite of myself, I was robbed of a lot of my memories. Ablation, extraction, excision... The dictionary contains only a few terms to designate loss and destruction. What is lost seems to have never existed.

"This memory from the end of my childhood, so alive in me still. The path that leads toward the hell of Azwélia... a leaden sky. Ancient pain, still fresh, I feel it transplanted into me like an enormous thorn.

"I remain for three days and three nights at Azwélia's. I was handed over by Fifie, defenseless. To move the sorceress to pity, I try sobbing;

I unsuccessfully attempt an alliance with her; I use all my knowledge to persuade her to allow herself to be corrupted.

'I'll steal Fifie's beautiful lace undergarments, as well as her beautiful gold watch and then bring them to you, if you won't force me to submit to your smelly baths and your incantations.'

"But Azwélia is like Fifie: unmovable, infinitely heartless. Just like Fifie, she doesn't bother with useless words. I subsequently learn that sorceresses never wear panties or jewellery and that Fifie has left me with her so that, with her magic, her good luck baths, she would transform me into a woman that no man could resist, in spite of my night-coloured skin.

"Azwélia's mission is to arm me with an implacable charm. Since there is nothing she can do to modify me physically, only magic can save me and, indirectly, save Fifie, who intends to get rid of me as fast as possible by giving me to the first taker.

"At the end of the third day at Azwélia's, I am groggy, stretched out on a mat, in her dirt floor hut. For the last ceremony, she has put on an indigo dress; a red scarf is tied around her waist. She spins like a top while chanting incantations. On her neck, in place of a necklace, a drunken snake sticks out its tongue frenetically and wriggles. I don't fear snakes. Thunder taught me how to catch them behind the head and squeeze them between the thumb and the index finger, until they fall, like emptied guts, at my feet.

"The voice of Azwélia, however, makes me tremble. It's a strange voice, like a high-pitched creaking, a squealing like the little rat's moans of pleasure in the cemetery. She is waving a flaming torch that she buries in her mouth from time to time, all the while swallowing a strong alcohol whose odour fills the hut. A lukewarm, sticky liquid drips between my legs; my head is dizzy. I wait to regain consciousness to try to act. I gather my strength to be able at the right moment to leap at the woman, grab her calves, and knock her off balance onto the mat. Once I have her down, I'll run away.

"Through a hole in the piece of sheet metal that serves as a roof, I see that dawn is near. Far away a drum rumbles; a stray rooster crows loudly. Some men are shouting at the oxen: ho! ha! The oxen low with their sad oxen voices. And I feel sadder than an animal at the slaughterhouse. I remember suddenly that we are on Dead End Plain. There are cane fields here. The oxen transport the cane to the factories where they make sugar. And the men pull on the yokes of the oxen and beat them violently with sticks, for no reason. I've often seen them pull the oxen, push them to make them move forward and beat them horribly, for nothing. If I had refused to follow Fifie, there's no doubt that she would have put a yoke on me and pulled me as far as Azwélia's.

"A little later, a bitter smell reaches me, the smell produced by burnt sugar cane. The characteristic smell of the Plain: the bagasse that they are burning. Because of the smell, I know where I am. Little by little I calm down and wonder what infernal drink has been able to make me sleep like this. What disgusting brews has Azwélia made me swallow? In what dirty silt am I lying? And why do I have such a stomach ache? So many useless questions.

"Busy whirling around, Azwélia doesn't even realize that I am watching her. The sorceress is in her own world; I am at her mercy. That's the day I realize I can't expect anything from Fifie. I must put an end to my foolish dreams of maternal tenderness and mourn forever the death of her love. I understand as well—and this frightens me for a moment— that I will never be able to forgive the one who brought me into the world for these three days at Azwélia's. These three days become the premises for a merciless war between Fifie and me. I'll have to learn to confront her, even if the weapons at my disposal are laughable," Emma concludes wearily, with a sort of unfurling of sadness in her whole body.

She leaves the window, straightens up her body, and goes over to the bed, where she lies down before pulling the covers over her face.

Nickolas of Sand and Shadow

Presently, I go to the hospital only two days a week. These long sessions with Emma empty me of all my substance. I continue to transcribe her words and to meet with Dr. MacLeod. I don't quite know why, but I notice that he is pre-occupied, impatient. When I arrived on the landing one morning, I caught him in deep conversation with another doctor. I think he's the boss, Dr. Dugasson. I caught the words 'police', 'interrogation', 'investigating officer.' I got the impression that they were hesitating so that I could enter the waiting room before they continued their conversation. Dr. Dugasson looks like a big pit bull, a Botero subject but with a gentle look, like that of a relaxed cat. That day I was thinking about Gilliane, who deplores my "idleness". In her opinion I am idle because, unlike her, I don't have to take care of two children without the help of a father. My mind is constantly roaming.

It's this idleness, probably, that leads me toward Nickolas Zankoffi, with whom a Friday evening ritual has been established. In the nostalgic mist of his years with Emma that he is sharing with me, we drink some very black tea while we listen to the blues that she loved so much. This man both worries and attracts me. When I think I understand him, he escapes me, like sand that slips between your fingers. He seems so alive and so unreal, a bit like a shadow. Time and life separate me from him; he is going to be fifty-five years old, he confided to me one evening, but sometimes I imagine that his nebulous life, his voice of distant tides and lands, will help me to interpret my existence. I get into a fight with myself every Friday evening about going to meet him. However, in spite of my doubts, I am always outside, walking sometimes without too much energy, sometimes very rapidly to avoid changing my mind, as though the act of hurrying allowed me to overcome my willpower. Gilliane, who complains about not seeing me anymore, claims that I have become imprisoned in a spiral formed by these two lunatics. I am just doing my work, I tell her, unconvinced. I meet Nickolas so he can confirm Emma's stories.

I wonder if it's the challenge, an unhealthy obsession, or loneliness that draws me, inexorably it seems, towards this man. Indeed, I have to admit that I am shocked to think that he never tried to discover what separated fact from fiction in Emma's life. Was it too difficult? Had he never thought of it? How can he claim to love her so much if what she was telling him about her past had so little importance for him? Even in the deepest part of his love, Emma's language must have remained impenetrable for him. Can one love someone without taming their language? All these questions caused me great dismay.

One day, it occurred to me to question Nickolas about his feelings toward the baby, little Lola, whom he must have held in his arms, whom he would have learned to fuss over. Wasn't she the fruit of that passion that he claimed he felt for Emma? He made that involuntary movement of his shoulders, I think, that instinctive movement which caused him to round his back, to slightly lower his head, while he brushed back with a graceful gesture a rebellious lock of hair.

"I was hoping, wishing that she would forget everything," he said. "I kept hoping that she would finally purge herself of all that past so that she could be completely mine. I wanted her to be new."

I insisted hungrily, for I saw that he was trying to avoid my question:

"What kind of child was Lola?"

"She was like all children. Resembled neither me nor Emma. Whenever I took her in my arms, she would start to scream. Emma pampered her a lot; she seemed to love her."

He was slipping away, slipping away. Impossible to catch him.

On returning home that evening, I called Gilliane to confide in her that I believed I had found the guilty party. She suggested that I take a very cold shower and have some chamomile tea. She was helping her son to finish a project on the Mayas; she hadn't finished preparing supper; her car was on the point of dying; she was sick of being in debt; and well, anything was possible, since I had described the man as being a lunatic! In any case... Her last words drowned in the sizzling of the meat that she was browning, and she said all that in a tone she tried to make sound patient, but it was both bitter and cutting.

I was disappointed in her welcome, in her way of looking at things. I listened to her, nevertheless. Gilliane needs an attentive ear. She believes that if she had known how to keep the father of her children, he would have filled this need. Gilliane believes a lot of things.

The following Friday, I am barely settled in front of the cup of tea that Nickolas has just poured for me before he starts to speak of

Emma. He comes and goes in a whirlwind of words, so much so that the apartment seems too small for his large frame. He gets up, touches and moves things without any reason at all. He makes me dizzy. I suddenly get the feeling that we are two animals caught in a trap: Nickolas clinging to the memory of Emma so as to not have to continue alone in his egocentric drifting, and me, my heart and my arms empty, looking desperately for an anchor. I listen to the man talk, still trying to persuade myself that if I am there, seated opposite him, it's because it's necessary, for Emma, for me to try to know more and to discover the guilty party.

I excuse myself and go to the bathroom to see my face in the mirror. I am so pale. The yellow of my blouse is reflected in my eyes. "Stop wearing that egg yellow so close to your face; you look like a sunflower," Gilliane often scoffs, who herself sports her brown skin with the greatest of pride. Gilliane looks more like an East Indian woman.

Without wanting to, I stop on my way back to glance at Nickolas's room, at that bed where he lived his most intense happiness with Emma. Suddenly, I feel his hand on my shoulder. It is warm and round, both firm and soft. I call on all my strength not to faint, right there, at his feet. "There is nothing more pitiful than the look of sexual desire or longing on a woman's face.

There is no elegance in hunger!" My mother's words resonate in me like a gong. In a quick movement, I distance myself from Nickolas.

Mother has always lived perched on her certainties like on stilts. Her vocabulary is studded with words such as 'transcendence', 'sublimation', 'dignity', 'elegance'. In her opinion, I am crazy to attach so much importance to romance. Women, whether they are white or black, are all in the same boat, she proclaims. There always comes a time when they must learn to get along without men. Her words sometimes crack like whiplashes. She started taking piano lessons at the age of sixty, doesn't miss a single concert, travels with Marielle, a friend who lives in the Gaspé. "Views of the sun rising above the peninsula are worth just as much as the most beautiful embraces in the arms of an Adonis," Mother had written me one summer when I had refused to go there with her and Marielle.

Without appearing to notice, still less feel offended, Nickolas comes back to sit at the table. While he again pours himself some tea, he continues, in a tone that is full of sadness:

"For Emma, any love relationship seemed suspicious, any love connection, a form of violence. 'I have in my body so many words born from suffering that pleasure can only be an illusion,' she would counter when I would get close to her."

Looking distressed, Nickolas has me read a sheet of paper containing the words: "Is it possible to banish the outrage of the lack of love and of the stigma, to grab, before throwing in the towel, the only chance left to me for my body and soul to finally be free and celebrate what has been the worst but also the best?" She had affixed it to the wall opposite the bed, he explained; then he continued:

"Once, after making love, I wrote her this poem."

He closes his eyes and, with a broken voice that confers a special intensity to his words, he starts reciting:

If your body has aged, it's more in the way of good wine. We will go as far as the highest peak of the hills of love, and I will drink you to the last drop. You were born with a star on your forehead and a burst of laughter for lovemaking. All your life, no matter how hard you look for a corset to hide that burst of laughter, all your life, no matter how hard you fight or try to run from yourself, my love will catch up with you. From here on, your life begins again with mine, and mine with yours. I don't want you to hide your star any more; I want to be guided by it to the end of time.

"The next day she answered me with another poem:

Because the history of my island has taken my life hostage, because history has made of me a mount that they muzzle, that they use and abuse, because we have always bowed our heads, because, as soon as I was born, my blood was dried up, drained off, I don't dare solicit the promise of future thrills.

"Generous and secret Emma," concludes Nickolas.

His hands form a cup as though moulding Emma. "I took her that evening," he said, speaking for himself alone, "I took her like one picks a rare flower."

After that visit to Nickolas Zankoffi, I decide not to see him any longer. Emma's pain seems to me to find in him too weak an echo, and I intend to act in solidarity with the demands that she is expressing in the middle of her madness. I resent the naïve responses that Nickolas offers for the barbarism described by Emma. They indicate, in my mind, a form of egocentrism, something artificial. His evasive answers about Emma's pregnancy and delivery, his lack of interest in Lola, come back to me. I wonder if he ever tried to understand Emma from the inside. Did he attempt just once, one little time, to try to put himself in her black woman's skin? I tell myself he is merely another of these men with dusty feet and a very animal sensuality who go from affair to affair, their hearts ringing hollow, their hands and their arms empty, their mouths full of words. Virtuoso of the word, does he only conceive of love through the prism of metaphysical discourses? Words with their vacuity, words and their deafening music, have replaced Emma in Nickolas's life. Very quickly he would forget Emma. The male sex organ has no memory, I repeat to myself so that I'll never forget it. For them, love is a torrent; the water flows with a roar. They are wildly in love, but like torrents they don't retain anything.

I resent myself above all for the attraction which that man exercises over me, for the turmoil that he creates in me, for his smiles that illuminate his face and make my heart race against my will. Have I not learned to regulate like a clock my most secret desires? To manage my urges, just like my bank account? A friend tells me that she finds unmatched pleasure in flirting, in seducing, which she does with a refinement worthy of the most artful courtesans. That's enough for her, she claims. She has learned to be free, a liberty which brings her the greatest of pleasures. Me, I tend rather to avoid the problem. Either I try to stay far away from men, following my mother's example, or else it's the complete opposite... The strongest desires, proclaims my mother, end up dying, just like flowers, dying their beautiful death. But the voice of Nickolas Zankoff doesn't go away. It carries me off in its currents and its wanderings.

The way he has of tipping his head, the fragrance of tobacco, and that roundness, that smoothness in his gestures. I decide that I hate him.

Mattie and Rosa

I took a few days off to rest up from Emma. I was all out of energy and resources. With my body exhausted from sleepless nights, I was walking about like a lost soul, and, in spite of my efforts, I was no longer able to dissociate my existence from that of Emma and Nickolas Zankoffi. As the days passed, my confusion increased. I was alternating between anger, despair, and an insane fear that the terrible images punctuating Emma's words might pursue me even in my sleep. I dreamt of going away to the end of the world, of jumping on a steed that would dash off and never stop.

I went back to my work nevertheless, with the idea of finishing it as fast as possible, to free myself. That morning, as always, I found Emma standing at the window. It was a rainy, dreary day. The rain water was ricocheting off the surface of the river, like pebbles thrown at high speed. She didn't bother to respond to the greeting of Dr. MacLeod, whom she hadn't even noticed for some time now. She gave me a sad smile, an atrocious smile, on a ravaged face that gazed at me in confusion and with an expression of suffering. Was she resentful that I had stayed away from her for the last fifteen days? She spoke in a monotone, her delivery very slow, as though she was already far away, very far from that room which looks out onto the river.

"A woman who talks too much makes as much noise as a cloud racing across the sky," she says looking at me intensely. "When we judge the noise to be of absolutely no use, we should swallow our tongues. You know, Flore, I've learned to appreciate your company."

That was the first time that she called me by my name.

"I know, I've been sort of rough on you. But, more than anything else, I would like to talk to you about several women. After them, all the sounds will be silent. In my throat, in my head, in my blood, there will be absolute silence," she said.

Her slow voice contrasted with her normal, fitful, angry delivery.

"You brought something fresh into my life, something that I can't put my finger on," she continued. "It's to thank you that I bequeath to you the lives of Mattie and Rosa. I am sure that you will get something out of this."

A thin smile now floated over her face, appearing, disappearing, like the moon behind the clouds. In vain I appealed to all the willpower I had left in me to find something to answer her. I wanted to tell her that I owed her a second life, in spite of the torment she had sown in me, but I wasn't able to choose the words. I was opening and closing my mouth desperately.

"Shh!" she said after a moment. "Don't ever forget, Flore, a woman who speaks, shouts, and screams in vain makes as much noise as a cloud. It's better to swallow our tongues, believe me, like our grandmothers on the boats."

As though in prayer, she closed her eyes for an instant, took a long breath and started her story:

"I was twelve years old and had a permanent taste of death in my mouth when I decided to leave Fifie. I took the road that leaves Grand-Lagon and I arrived at dawn at Moussambé. I found refuge in the home of a woman called Mattie, a cousin of my deceased grandmother Rosa. Grandmother had died five years earlier; Mattie had taken care of her until the end. Neither Fifie nor Grazie had gone to her funeral.

"Just as she had welcomed my grandmother when life had come crashing down on her, Mattie welcomed me into her home. It seemed like she was expecting me, like it had been written that one day I would arrive at her house, with my wrinkled little Indian-cotton dress and my bashed-in suitcase, and Thunder right on my heels. I was safe; I was sure neither Fifie nor

Aunt Grazie would come to search for me. I felt like a raft, drifting, alone on the immensity of the ocean. At that point in my life, I swear, my heart was bleeding. I spent whole nights calling for Fifie with all my strength, begging her to give me a little space in her life. The compassion and tenderness that filled Mattie's eyes and that she showered on me unsparingly, all her care and attention, were not sufficient to fill the void in me. I had come to Mattie with a single idea in my mind: to find out everything about my grandmother's life, to find the life lines that Fifie refused to hold out to me to help me find my way.

'Since Fifie couldn't understand, she closed her heart to you,' Mattie attempted to explain. 'To survive we often have no other choice. When the pain is too harsh, when it becomes too strong, we lose the meaning of things. There are pains that we manage to withstand because we understand them; we know where they come from. But the suffering that inhabits us because of what we are, the suffering that inhabits us because the world pushes us aside to the extent of making us hate our own flesh, is difficult to understand and accept, Emma. It's not surprising that madness is waiting for us at the end of that tunnel, and it's then that we destroy our own flesh, because we fear for it, we know what awaits it.

'To live in the skin of a black woman is to live permanently in a night without stars,' Mattie would say. 'A dense night that weighs on us like a burden. That's why we want to get rid of it, to distance ourselves from it without looking back. We want to run away from our black woman's skin like one shuns the night and its demons. Thus, we abandon our own people; we kill our children; and we flee even from our own shadow.

'God created the day and the night. He also created the day animals and those of the dark. And we, the dark women, we are the ones that are attacked by life and everything violent that it contains. Life abuses us with noisy brutality. Who can tell me when,' Mattie would say as her voice got louder, 'when, since the world began, has life dressed us in lace and silk? You mustn't be mad at Fifie, my little one, in spite of everything, you can't be mad at her. The evil your mother is suffering from comes from far away. It flows in our veins; we swallow it with the first mouthful of our mothers' milk.'

"Each day with Mattie was a long apprenticeship. Just as I had roamed over the plains, entered the caves, climbed the mountains with Thunder, I was now exploring with Mattie the sinuous contours of human beings. She was teaching me to discover the places of refuge where the soul could hide, so that all that remained was the appearance of my woman's body, this ebony body, the object of lust and repulsion, of both desire and hate.

'These attitudes regarding our bodies, our skin, have marked out our destiny,' Mattie would often say with a strange smile. 'It's for that reason that we have learned not to waste time in a vain quest for happiness. But, even in our existences that are nothing but bitterness, we never approach life as though we are going through an ordeal. Better to use our strength to deflect the arrows that destiny directs at us.' That is what Mattie was teaching me, this woman who could neither read nor write.

"Paradoxically, it's from her that I got my passion for learning, Flore. As Mattie used to say, it was a way of 'deflecting the arrows of destiny, because only what is well rooted in your head can't mislead you.' The high school was located many miles from the village; I would wake up before dawn to get there. Mattie didn't shrink from any sacrifice to buy me the books I needed. She would pick them up, caress them, smell them, with a smile of contentment in the corner of her eyes. I ran off with all the prizes; and of course I made the other students jealous.

"Living with Mattie was like living in a big book, a book that she constructed each day, page after page, and in which I discovered the arabesques and the meanderings of human souls.

It's in this book that I discovered some amazing lives: those of Béa, the mother of my grandfather, Baptiste, and Rosa, my maternal grandmother.

"Mattie lived alone. She had been living alone since the departure of Baptiste and Grandmother Rosa. She described Baptiste, my grandmother's husband, as a tall black man with gentle eyes and a voice like a caress. She emphasized that he was nothing like those phantoms of misfortune who haunt our island, walking from house to house to dump their eggs in the entrails of our black women and run away, their pants all rumpled. No, Baptiste's knowledge of women was only what his mother had taught him. Béa was a black woman whose skin was sprinkled with freckles. She was a woman whose hands and eyes were always moving. She was reborn with every dawn. She laughed at lost keys, opened every door, always approached new shores saying 'make a place for me, here I am!' She never mourned her past lives, for she knew that nothing is ever permanent for women. She had lots of arms, so many arms, to work all the paths, the fields through which she passed. All that, she had bequeathed it to her son, that man Baptiste, the one who had known how to bring some sweetness to Rosa's existence, as though to prove that in spite of everything, in spite of the hell of the plantations, some of them had succeeded in salvaging the strength to exist. 'Don't be satisfied with watching life pass you by,' was Baptiste's motto, the motto that he received from Béa, his mother, that black woman who had forgotten nothing of the voyage of her ancestors, from the Diola country to the cane fields in the island.

"To tell you the truth, Flore, Mattie did everything possible to help me avoid what she designated as 'the curse'. But, somewhere, I flinched. The road was too long, I think, the race too desperate. One day, I remember, Mattie said to me:

'On destiny's path there are trees whose fruit has a bitter peel but a juicy interior, sweet and soft like a custard apple...'

'Yet another one of those fruits which is not intended for our lips, Mattie,' I interrupted.

'That's what your Grandmother Rosa said. She talked just like you. But, with that big man's laugh which warms you up like a good grog, Baptiste answered her: "a true black woman takes the bitter peel, the defect, and prepares it in such a way that it is the most delicious dish in the world!"

"Baptiste looked with love on everything, on all that came from Rosa. A strong tenderness united them, and, that, no one understood. As though, because we ourselves had been given a rough time, we should in turn give each other a rough time. As if that period of slave owners, that period of cane production, should never end.

"At that instant in her tale, Mattie's face would become luminous with a light that made her skin shine. Tiny little shivers would go through her whole body.

'Well no, little girl,' she would suddenly lower her voice, which was now only a sadly hummed song—'well no, Baptiste had sworn that his Rosa would be his past, his present, his future. Days and nights were the same for them. They were no longer but a single body, a single soul. For that they have never been forgiven. And believe it or not, little girl, it was above all your grandmother that people envied. They resented her for that beautiful loaf of life which satisfied her hunger. That's what it is, Emma; no one forgives a blue-skinned black woman for having a life like a wide well-cleared path before her. You're supposed to move ahead through brambles and thickets, to roam the hills, to grab your daily bread out of the jaws of mad dogs! Oh yes, that's how it is! You are supposed to toil, howl louder than wolves, fall down, and crawl on your knees, on your backside!

'Grand-Lagon, this bit of land crouching in the middle of the ocean, Grand-Lagon, we mustn't be afraid to say it, is a cursed land, Emma. This water that has washed it since the day it was born, this water, with its blue so blue, hides centuries of blood vomited from the holds of the slave ships, blood from all the blacks that were thrown overboard. That's how the curse arrived. It infiltrated the water of our rivers, the water that we drink, it mixed with our blood, spoiled it. Oh, little one. Everything that you are making me relive now,' she said angrily, 'all that makes me sick!' That's what Mattie said, and a large streak of pain crossed her face. 'But how to avoid telling you all this since you won't escape it? The curse pursues us, Emma, as did the dogs loosed on our trail on the plantations in the old days. It dogs us, panting behind us. It's there, attached to us; it's perhaps the curse which makes our hips heavy, who knows?'

'But me, I don't have hips, Mattie!' I complained. 'At school the girls call me pastry board. They say that in addition to my blue skin, I am shaped all of a piece and because of that no man will ever want me.'

'Let them talk, my Emma, let them talk, and so much the worse for the men who won't want you... When the blacks found shelter in the woods, do you think that laughter was absent?' continued Mattie. 'No, Emma. That's why our lips are so big. To store laughter, which is a feast of the body. Look at me; you can count the teeth I have left and my laugh is no worse, believe me.'

"Mattie broke out in an immense burst of laughter that made her whole body move. I laughed and Mattie laughed with me, for she still loved to laugh, Mattie did. She's the one who taught me the joy of rounds of laughter that ride the body, go up and down the chest. Alas, I no longer know how to laugh, Flore."

I was startled. Drowned in Emma's story, only my body had been present in the room. As for Dr. MacLeod, with his eyes half closed, he seemed to be inert, in a strange torpor. Had we both developed a taste for that atmosphere of fabulous lunacy which caused us to fall head over heels into a film of another epoch?

"For me, Mattie revisited over and over again her childhood with my grandmother Rosa. She spoke to me of the beginning of their life together, of Rosa and Baptiste. From that union with a man coveted by all the women in Grand-Lagon, whether of marriageable age or not, were born two beauties, Fifie and Grazie, two mixed-race blondes, whose faces had been been sculpted in pure gold.

'The birth of these girls constituted an extraordinary event at Grand-Lagon,' explained Mattie. 'For ten days, people flocked to Rosa's to see up close that black woman with her blue skin and her two kids, the colour of fire, hanging onto her breasts. Two *chabines* with eyes of molten gold. Some people made the sign of the cross, opening wide their distraught eyes, then they took off. Many laughed while hiding their faces behind their handkerchiefs, but the boldest didn't even wait until they had left the house before starting to gossip.

'She has played him for a fool! Or else black people are making great miracles now. Come on! Who will make me believe that they're from him?'

'But you don't get it,' laughed a gossiper. 'It's his thing, you know, his thing there,' she laughed as though her belly would burst. 'What comes out of his thing, it's molten gold. And he does it so well that she lays two at a time!'

"The birth of these two gilded daughters, sprung from her black womb, accelerated Rosa's fall. Baptiste didn't understand how Rosa had been able to betray him like that. Where did these little yellow-haired devils come from who resembled neither him nor Béa, his black mother? How could they have sprouted from his body the colour of the night, this body without one drop of sunlight under his skin?

"The years passed quickly and dug the tomb of Rosa and Baptiste. He was still kind to her. But she felt that he was somewhere else, like a body of water that withdraws inexorably. In the house, his big body was restless or else he was crushed, gathered up into himself, packed tight like a package of clothes in a corner. Often, she had to go to get him by the sea, on the shore.

She found him seated, his eyes riveted, floating, on the waves. She would call him; he would turn his head slowly, his face unshaven and bony. It seemed like he barely recognized her. He was no longer the same Baptiste.

"In his gestures something was being born that she didn't understand, that frightened her, like a large wind that wanted to destroy every-thing in its path. Rosa, who, since the first day of her marriage, when her body had melted into Baptiste's, Rosa who knew how to read every-thing in his thoughts, stood there at his side, her arms dangling, no longer understanding any-thing, not being able to say anything.

"Then, he moved away with large steps. He never cast a single glance at his daughters, who were growing tall like bamboo stalks, with skin full of sun, a flame of arrogance and content-ment growing each day behind their pupils.

"Soon, Baptiste's steps went totally astray in the night of Grand-Lagon. He no longer came home. Time went by for Rosa in a sort of mad-ness, listening to the cuckoos, the canaries and other chimeras beating their wings. Like a mad-woman, she struggled with the desires of her body and her soul which called out to Baptiste with all their strength. 'Emma, if you only knew! But you are much too young to compre-hend all that and I pray to heaven that it removes such torments from your path. I went down on my knees and implored God to send Baptiste back to Rosa, for a little moment, only an instant, a little transitory gentleness.'

'To think that Baptiste could have changed her life, the life of a woman the colour of the night... When I think about it, oh, when I think about it... ' Mattie shook her head sorrowfully.

"At Grand-Lagon, when they realized that Baptiste was wandering here and there like a wild old black man, without purpose and without ties, when they realized that henceforth he was like a dog without a master, that he had even forgotten the way to Rosa's, they were carried away in rejoicing... She was falling off her pedestal, that Rosa! Enough playing the great lady! After all, who did she think she was to keep a man? Just a woman with blue skin, skin without a glimmer of light, for whom existence should be only some dreams. That's what people were thinking. And that's what we've had to struggle against since the beginning of time.'

"And there, I would like so much for you to answer me," Emma called on me once again. "Isn't that the same thing they thought when they rejected my thesis? Who does she think she is to be aspiring to take a turn at writing history? What does she want to prove? By what right?"

She glanced askance at Dr. MacLeod and cleared her throat at length, before taking up her story again.

"In the market, when the gossips saw Rosa arrive, they started to snicker and to whisper that so and so had seen him, this very same Baptiste, here and there, his pants swinging between his legs. He had been seen coming out of Corinne's, Nella's, or Maria's. He had become like the others, they concluded with satisfaction.

"It's with Mattie that I began to understand our history and what had taken place on the slave ships. Trembling, she disclosed to me these episodes of the life of one woman or the other, episodes she linked, as others had done before her, to the torments inherited from sugar cane slavery. But after I left Mattie, my thirst to understand became still stronger. I searched in the great books. I searched so much, Flore, if you only knew all that I've read. For many years I looked and looked, to discover the source of that horror and that hate. The books made me crazy, believe me. In spite of everything, I wanted to open up my brain in order to hide them in it. While I was working on that thesis that they used as toilet paper, there were nights on end that I couldn't sleep. I went out into the streets to take my black woman's rage for a walk, on the docks of Nantes, of Bordeaux, and La Rochelle. I stopped passersby, most often drunkards, to ask them if they knew how much sugar, how much blood, how many slaves, how much black women's milk had been needed to construct just one European city."

With her eyes closed, as though to soften the words she was pronouncing, Emma talked, and as her voice rolled on, her body emptied itself of these images thrust up from the depths of an ancient memory, words extracted from archives buried in her entrails.

"One day, I will talk to you in detail about the slave ships," she promises me. "Another day. Then you will understand, you will understand everything. It's in the holds that everything was written, in the folds of the sea, in the wind gorged on salt, and in that smell of blood. A foul smell, present everywhere, but that people pretend not to recognize, still envelops the island. So much blood, too much blood," she moans.

"We were more than a hundred thousand, a hundred thousand, two hundred thousand, three hundred thousand. Trails of blood, streams of blood, rivers and oceans of blood. Our history is written in blood, and we will be wading in blood eternally."

At this point in her story, Emma seemed so exhausted that Dr. MacLeod himself intervened to put an end to the session. Without protesting, she let us take leave of her. She felt so weak that she agreed to take my arm to get back to her bed.

Today Emma takes up her story where she had left off two days before, as though she had never taken a break.

"Mattie worshipped our history and our dreams faithfully, religiously. Everything, for her, was a reason to evoke our history; everything, it seems, was a reason to maintain the lifeline and to plant in me her memories, those of grandmother Rosa, everything Mattie knew about her, about her life, about the lives of all the other women, those before them and those before me.

'Even when our history carries along nothing but bitterness,' said Mattie, 'it's necessary to know how to sustain it. Our history is sometimes a squall, an undertow, or sand that traps us. But it is also a branch to which we can cling when the tides are too strong.'

"Mattie had made it a habit to open the windows of her dreams to me. That's what she would say when she decided to relate them to me.

'A dream never comes alone, little one. It never comes by chance, like an animal that loses its way and goes astray. A dream is sent to us. It's a key that is given to us to put all the pieces in place. Life cuts us up into little pieces, but if we take the time to look into our dreams, we can find meaning even in the crumbs. Don't forget, Emma, that those who are no longer near us know all the innermost secrets of our suffering.

They come in our dreams to help us find the scattered pieces.'

"I often didn't understand Mattie's words. But I described to her all the dreams in which Fifie hugged me so tight that I melted into her, that I became one with her. I told Mattie my main, constant dream, the one in which the earth opened and swallowed me up. Her voice broke and she shuddered when she answered me.

'I tell you, little one, this big dream worries me; it worries me terribly!'

"She seemed to think for a moment; then she went on.

'Dreams where everything is destroyed frighten me, Emma. It is important to have something to cling to. We have been destroyed so many times, in the slave ships, in the fields. We have to struggle, Emma, in order to defy destruction; we have to struggle continuously to save our souls. In this dream, you destroy everything. It's no longer a question of surviving. This is a dream of tempests, gales, and confrontations. A dream where I see a lot of blood. Where are you going to hide, little one? I can't see where.'

"She spoke these words so seriously that it was my turn to shudder.

"From Mattie I learned that when Grandmother Rosa left Grand-Lagon, Fifie and

Grazie had refused to follow her. Mattie at first said that she had never understood their reasons, then, sadly, she confessed: it was to be far from their mother, far from her night-coloured skin. You understand, that is what destruction is: when your own flesh and blood feel obliged to reject you, in order to feel that they exist.

"At the time of Baptiste's final departure, Fifie and Grazie were twelve years old. 'Ah, if you only knew, Emma, all the grief they gave Rosa!' Mattie told me. Grazie stared at her one day with her eyes of molten gold, then she spit on the ground: 'How could a blue-skinned woman have brought into the world a girl like me?' Day after day, Rosa thought long and hard; how had that been able to happen, why her? Which of her ancestors, she wondered, had been jumped by some white demon in heat; and in which hell: the cane, the cotton, or the coffee plantation? Why had her belly vomited up that insult so many years later? A double insult since there were two of them. Everywhere she looked in the house she bumped into their eyes of molten gold. It was phantasmagoric; she couldn't even manage to tell them one from another. They saw her turmoil and acted in a way that doubled her torment.

"Five years after the departure of Baptiste, Rosa had discovered everything, had learned everything there was to know about suffering.

'But she struggled,' continued Mattie, closing her eyes very tightly and making little gestures with her hand, as though she were attempting to chase away bad memories. 'She had eventually put back in place certain pieces of her life. One morning, she escaped from her chains. She left Grand-Lagon.

'The years passed without news from her daughters. Only rumours. She heard that the minds and the hands of all the shoeless black men on the island were taken up with the bodies of Grazie and Fifie, whom they would stand in line day and night to meet. Without a word, Rosa's daughters would lie down, submissive to all those who walked into the house of their father, Baptiste, into the house he had built with his own hands back in the days when they were transforming everything they touched into impetuous happiness.

'Fifie and Grazie didn't know how to live inside their inside-out skins. They floated about, weren't tied to any perch, weren't tied up to any dock. So, they offered that skin to all comers, that skin, an envelope without a soul. Fifie was struck doubly hard. The haughtiness, the arrogance, the vainness of both of them, all of that was wiped out by you, Emma, swallowed up in your blood, the blackest blood, the purest asphalt, infiltrated into the veins of your mother by one of those louts.

'I tell you all that, Emma, because it's the truth,' Mattie added eventually, 'but I couldn't explain to you why that happened. Ah, my little Emma! Those days of shame, confusion, and humiliation almost got the better of my Rosa. She went about like an uprooted tree, aimlessly, a tree traversed to its roots by the wind. Behind her back, people whispered. Everyone had an explanation. Then—as she told me— one night three women came to visit her. They were Cécile, the eternal maroon, Béa, Baptiste's mother, and Kilima, the first of her lineage: in other words, the first one of all our ancestors to arrive on the island.'

'Where did all those women come from, Mattie? Hadn't they been dead for centuries?' I asked her pointedly.

"Mattie never said the women who had made the big voyage were dead, but that they had fallen down; a way of saying that she didn't accept their absence or their defeat, because, for Mattie, a woman was a warrior. A warrior doesn't die. She has the duty to pick herself up in order to continue the fight. Mattie had an impressive repertoire of tales in which a woman warrior always gets back up and, in order to walk, borrows the feet and legs of those being born. That's why women would also take the names of those who had fallen, like one carries on with secrets, like one puts on old clothes.

That's why, in spite of herself, Fifie had called me Emma, the name of her own grandmother.

'In a paling fence, the new poles always lean against the old ones,' Mattie continued, so that I would understand that we black women, when we die, we can't go away forever. 'We don't have that right,' she would say, 'since those who remain behind are still in need of us. Don't you know that on the ships, we held hands to throw ourselves into the waves and avoid the chains?'

"But Fifie will never come for me, even after her death."

'Who are you to claim to understand everything?'

"To answer me Mattie had used a tone and accents that I did not recognize. I think she resented my not understanding that Fifie had been caught in that same mechanism as well; just like me, crushed by the same gearwheel.

'Those women formed a circle around Rosa. All three wore sparkling white garments. Their snowy hair made lilac-coloured halos around their faces. It was both strange and beautiful, your grandmother told me. She hadn't been afraid. She asked them very simply what they were doing there. "You must know why we have come," Kilima answered her.

'They were in the middle of the ocean. Behind them was the outline of the tall mountains, La Selle and Les Gabions. One after the other, they sprinkled your grandmother with water and said to her: "A black woman who lets them take all of her soul isn't a black woman, Rosa. She's a prostrate woman! Pick yourself up! That's our request! What energy will you have for the voyage back to Guinea? Do you know how many crossroads you still have to negotiate? It's impossible to count them. Pick yourself up, Rosa Guinea," they order her again. "We are not in the habit of coming to look for those women who allow life to dispossess them of their souls."

'Suddenly, Cécile rose up into the air. She had no feet. She showed her arms to Rosa. No hands either. She was hitting the air with her four stumps. That's when your grandmother remembered Cécile's story, the Bantu woman Cécile, the maroon for all times, the eternal maroon. With your grandmother, that night, I went back in time. But I'll tell you all about that another time,' Mattie told me that day. 'Don't forget, a woman who talks too much makes as much noise as a cloud in the sky.' That's how, every evening, Mattie closed the big book about the women from the country of Guinea.

'It's after that vision that Rosa put an end to her drifting. She gave to the ocean,' Mattie told me, 'that immense distress that she had carried along with her everywhere. It was no longer a question of wanting to die. She kept herself standing tall in life. She had put death underneath her mattress, telling it to wait until she had finished her sparkling white garment for her voyage, to wait until she had learned everything about her life, so that I, in turn, could pass it on to you.'"

Kilima

Just as Emma had to wait for Mattie to continue her story, Dr. MacLeod and I had to wait
more than a week before Emma came back to
hers. Whenever we went into her room, she
stayed in bed, with the covers pulled up to her
chin, not answering us, not even opening her
eyes. Only once did she open her mouth to tell
us in one gasp:

"Go away, you jackals!"

I was flabbergasted. Dr. MacLeod reassured
me:

"Don't be upset, Flore. This won't last."

In fact, today, fresh and in good spirits, Emma
picks up her story as usual, right where she has
left off, which always surprises the doctor.

"So it's because of Mattie," Emma points
out, "that I know the destinies of the women of
my lineage, the lives of Kilima, my Bantu ancestor, and of Cécile ,who was not part of the same
clan but acted as Kilima's mother when she
arrived as a child on the Count plantation on the
island of Saint-Domingue. Kilima gave birth to

Emma, whose name I bear, then came Rosa, then another Emma, then another Rosa, my grandmother, whose story you already know.

"I, for my part, described to Mattie a universe that she had never known: the life in the great books of paper, as she called them. 'Today one can cheat destiny with education; in my time, that wasn't possible.' Mattie encouraged me in my school work. She had so many dreams for me. Sometimes, when I was doing my homework, she would watch me for hours seated on a little bench. She would open my books and look at the letters like one looks at pictures.

"Life was less bitter with Mattie, though. I began to hope that her dreams would bear fruit, that the path ahead of me would open onto a slightly wider one than had been the case with my grandmother Rosa. I used to dream with my eyes open, and, without knowing why, I would be gripped by despair; the whole inside of my body would feel frozen. Fear would sneak under my eyelids at night. I was afraid of the day that would come when I would have to leave Mattie and set out alone in life. 'It wouldn't be fair to keep you, Emma,' Mattie insisted, 'you must confront destiny, be ready to meet it; don't forget.' But destiny, as everybody knows, does whatever it feels like doing. It had already stolen Thunder from me. That happened one evening when I was returning from school; I found him on the porch. Surprised at not seeing him rush toward me, I knelt down to embrace him. He was rigid like the trunk of a tree. His tongue was hanging out like a damp sock; flies were buzzing all around him. That was the first time I really cried. The tears I shed sank into his fur as I tried unsuccessfully to lift him. I wasn't crying out loud; I was weeping silently. Mattie didn't stop me; then in the dark she helped me to dig a grave. I still occasionally wake up with a start because I suddenly sense his musky dog smell.

"I finished high school very fast and got a scholarship after a year spent in the capital, at the Faculty of Ethnology. Every weekend, I would go home to be with Mattie. One day, however, I had to leave her. That scholarship was going to let me continue my education in faraway countries, as she would say, very satisfied. I chose France, a country to which I felt no particular tie except that History had willed that I get my education in its language. Deep down, however, my project was taking shape: to examine the routes taken in the old days by the big ships.

"Mattie had taught me this song from the other side of the ocean, which the women had saved from the holds of the slave ships:

Kilima changu kidogo, my little hill
Kitu changu kidogo, my little thing

Mtoto mdogo, my tiny little child
Inakua usiku, the night comes
Wewe malayika wangu, my guardian angel
I carried her song off with me."

This morning, Emma has put back on her lilac-coloured poplin smock. Her skin looks bluer than ever.

"I didn't sleep a wink last night," she admits to me, "but, even though I feel tired, I must talk to you about Kilima."

"It's July," she starts, "the month of the rainy season and heat waves. It's nighttime, but much too hot to go to bed. The night is sizzling and crackling like the day. It crackles from the blazing heat of the sun that, all day long, has been beating down on us without respite. Over on the hill, the wind is bending the trees as they are reciting their prayers. The summer nights are so long. To elude them, we fill them with secrets and words. Nights are the old books of our memory. They start when the sun dips behind the hills, when everything slows down and the unchained voice of a banjo or a harmonica reaches us. As soon as the voice of the drum rises in the distance in the night, I huddle up against Mattie. I feel her smooth skin there on her forearm. I snuggle up still closer to her. I feel like I am caressing my own arm, touching a part of my own flesh. The voices of the drums resound like a call launched from the top of the mountains to raise up the armies of fallen women. I hear them advancing.

"In the feeble light, I see Mattie dampen her dried lips with her tongue. I am thirteen years old, but I am so small that Mattie still sits me on her knees to braid my hair. Even when the braids are perfect, with all the little strands of hair properly stuck to each other, she undoes them each evening, rolls them between her thumb and index finger before braiding them again. Sometimes she follows the same pattern; sometimes she designs another route. While she is moistening her lips, while she is moving her fingers, Mattie talks. She knows the lives of all the women of our area. She can talk for the whole night. She pities those whose souls have remained in prison, those who don't know how to protect themselves, who don't know how to be maroons, who let themselves be deprived of everything.

'They can imprison your body, little one,' she tells me, while pulling on my braids as on the bridle of a horse, 'but promise me that your soul will always be free like a bird. You can throw it up into the clouds, hang it on the highest branch, on the highest mountain peak, and lis-ten to it talk to you from anywhere when you are alone. Too many women don't know that they have a soul. When their body is thought of as road dust to be spit on, tell me, little one—in spite of your youth, I am sure that you know it as well as I do—well then, when all that happens to us, when our eyes cannot hold back our tears, well then, yes, our soul leaves us, it is carried off in our tears, it is washed away like sediment in a storm. Then we walk about like zombies, with madness in our eyes and in our guts.'

"That hairdressing session is a ritual that precedes the night. It's also my hour of lessons with Mattie. I review every day: the first woman was called Kilima, she had been torn away from her mother Malayika, then sold to the slavers. On the island, she gave birth to Emma, then Emma to Rosa and Rosa to Emma, then Emma to your grandmother Rosa, then came Fifie, and again Emma. And in my veins flows that same blood.

"The heat is sticky. It encloses us; I perspire as if I were in a cocoon. Mattie talks; she tells me similar stories about those women who, because of their suffering, lose their souls and are transformed into lost souls. One of them, Célanie, roamed all over the place like a crazy ant.

'Well,' says Mattie, 'one day Célanie met a horse, a beautiful white horse. It had only two legs, but its shoes made the same noise as those who have four, you know: *giddyup, giddyup, gid-*

dyup... As quickly as she could say it, whoop, memory-less Célanie jumped up onto the saddle and the horse carried her off. She was never heard from again.'

"I wait a few minutes, then I ask Mattie what one does to distinguish horses with two legs from those with four, if their galloping makes the same noise.

'All you have to do is let your soul do the looking, my child. It alone knows the truth.'

"As she talks, Mattie slowly waves a square of cardboard close to her face. At Moussambé, the rain never manages to chase away the heat.

"When Mattie tells her story," Emma explains, "she takes lengthy breaks, as though she were concentrating on carefully choosing among the memories that are unfolding within her." That makes me think that Emma is simply trying to let me know that, with her slow delivery, her hesitations, she in turn is carefully choosing among the to-ings and fro-ings of the story which she relives endlessly.

"'What is worse than a woman's body without its memory, Emma?' Mattie asks me that evening. 'Little one,' she says, 'before long, I will be leaving. But, after me, you will pass on this memory.'

"When I look like I am about to protest, she stops me by putting her hand over my mouth. She plunges her gray eyes into mine, two little openings behind which appear her pupils, like two branding irons.

'Everything started with Kilima,' Mattie then begins. 'With Kilima, because that is the name of our ancestor, the first of our forbears taken away by the slave traders. Kilima, in Swahili, means 'mountain'. That's the name the elders gave her the day she was born. There was only one thing she remembered from her past life: the voice of her mother, Malayika; that voice, like the bite of a beast whose violent poison had seeped into her. The voice of her mother, screaming on the shore, while the slave ship cuts through the water, tearing open the limpid blue of the ocean. The ship sails away, carrying off in its flanks its cargo of ebony wood, including Kilima. The ship leaves and Malayika screams, screams her soul out onto the beach.

'In Swahili, Malayika means guardian angel.

'Can anyone let out such a scream and stay alive, my child?'

'No, Mattie.'

'You do understand. One cannot let out such a scream and stay alive, the child Kilima told herself. For sure, her mother must have expelled her soul in that scream. She no longer had any doubt: that voice which had rooted itself in her was the soul of her mother, which had left her body on the shore to accompany her daughter.

'The crossing on this slave ship was merciless, nothing but a continuous roaring, a horrible bellowing which rose from the belly of the ship, heard only by the ocean. Crouched in a corner of the hold, Kilima let herself be rocked by the lapping of the water, while the voice that she alone could hear was whispering to her that she was only at the beginning of these long voyages of misery.

'The morning following her arrival on the island, the Count, a squat, short-legged little man, baptized her. He poured a pitcher of cold water onto her head and slapped her loudly on each cheek, as was the custom, leaving stripes on the mauve skin of her face, all the while shouting at her to repeat three times: *Rosa, Rosa, Rosa*. At that moment, a big black cloud swept down on Kilima. She swallowed her tongue and swore to never ever pronounce a single word in the presence of others, as long as she remained a slave. And she never answered when she was called by this new name.

'As the only one in charge, the Count didn't burden himself with the presence of a priest. He baptized his slaves himself. Short, easy-to-remember names. Names that he could shout in a single breath, one or two syllables spit out of his mouth like a seed, that cracked like the blows of a whip: Léa, Rosa, Tom, Jim, Betty, Sara, Paul, Béa, Zabeth...

'On her wan skin, dulled by bad treatment and by the sorrow that was consuming her, Kilima bore for a long time the marks of the Count's five fingers. That same week, he brand-ed her with a hot iron: a mark on the left cheek, the *C* of the word 'Count,' like a crescent moon.

'The unofficial story, which filtered in from the neighbouring plantations, had it that this notorious Count was in fact merely a common assassin, from the prisons of Paris. The whites from France had seized that island to appropri-ate everything that was there. In return, they were dumping onto the island armfuls of every-thing that was rotten in their country. And that rot set about swelling in the bellies of the women they were bringing in by boat from the lands on the other side of the ocean. During the crossing, which lasted for months and months, the sailors got drunk, then went down into the holds and took the women without even letting them out of their heavy chains.

'All that is very complicated, little Emma,' sighed Mattie. 'But you have to learn it, for that's how everything started. As soon as the boats docked, hardly had the chains been removed from their feet, than the blacks, both men and women, were sent to the fields. And there, whites, blacks, less-white whites, less-black blacks, all threw themselves on the night-coloured women, unbidden, as though they were drawing water from the river to quench their thirst.

'I try sometimes to console myself by telling myself that this period was an accident, since accidents, misfortunes and all the calamities which befall good Christians don't beat the drum to announce their arrival. But one either recovers from an accident or one dies. We didn't die, that's the truth, but here we are, forever crippled.

'These new rich lands that the whites named colonies were sheltering so many horrors under their paradisal finery that they couldn't be considered to be just more accidents. God himself, when he created the world, couldn't avoid accidents, for didn't it happen that we were catapulted into the middle of hell?

'That's how the women used to talk in the old days, our ancestors, all those who learned to retain from a place only its imprint on the balls of their feet and to restrict their unhappy memories to the very edge of their hearts.'"

"Mattie also said that we needed to constantly hunt down the obscenity that suffering carries with it. Alas, this obscenity, it seems to me, too often encircles us, strips us of what can be so precious and so human, transforms us into filthy vultures, obliges us to put our entire hand into the wound. That's certainly what I am doing, isn't it, Flore?"

With her eyes Emma seemed to be questioning me, and, since I gave her no answer, she added:

"I would love to escape obscenity, but suffering and obscenity often go together, Flore. I'm sorry, they often go together." She exhales an immense sigh and, once again, straightens herself up before diving back into her story.

" 'Emma,' Mattie added, 'you are the last of the line, the last of the daughters and granddaughters of Kilima. Fifie, your mother, is the next-to-last and you the last. After you, there won't be anyone.'

'How do you know?' I asked her, apprehensively.

'I don't know, little one. I don't know,' Mattie repeated, visibly upset as well. 'I don't think I am wrong. You won't have anyone to pass the life line on to. But, before that, you will be rid of all the bitterness that we carry in our veins. As though in a very ancient dream, you will repeat the deeds of the women of the clan, the efforts they made to shelter their children from the garrotes that choked them in the holds of the slave ships and in the fields of sugar cane. All that isn't very clear deep inside me. There is a kind of mauve cloud, a big cloud that makes everything less clear. Forgive me, little one, but sometimes I see bad omens. It's because of these dreams that you're having, your dreams of tempests and big winds. Your dreams trouble me.

'Kilima's clan's last drop of blood, deported to the New World, will be extinguished with you, like an eye that closes. It will be extinguished with you, my daughter,' Mattie repeated softly that night, as though to convince herself of what to her seemed all too true: 'It will be extinguished in a great din.'"

"What happens to our blood when we die, Flore?" Emma, who suddenly seems to remember my presence, asks me.

I shrug my shoulders. Once more, I don't know what to say. For the past little while, Emma hasn't been the least bit aggressive toward me anymore. She smiles at me sadly when I arrive, offers me a chair, helps me to get settled. As for Dr. MacLeod, he no longer exists for her. Sometimes she reads a poem that she has written during the night. Long texts, full of screams, shrieks and children's bodies, of sirens, of ships departing, of bruised and torn ebony bodies.

"Our blood," she continues, without waiting for my answer; "something tells me that it leaves our bodies in large bitter bubbles and angrily seeps into the entrails of the earth to return to the path from which it's been diverted. When everything is finished, my blood will rejoin that of Kilima, Rosa, the Emma who came before me, and the others."

"On the Count plantation, they used to say that Kilima was crazy.

'She is raving mad, that Kilima. And to cure her, believe me, we should chain her to the base of the big breadfruit tree and let the enormous fruits knock her out. That'll do it. When she gets hit on the head, it will free her tongue and all the devils that she has brought with her from her bush!'

'I forbid you to talk like that, Canot. What rotting-hole do you come from, you scoundrel?'

"She leaps to her feet, the woman who speaks these words, and, as she motions in grand gestures with her hand, her voice becomes more threatening."

I feel like I am watching a play, a theatrical production, where Emma plays all the roles, for she gets up and attempts to mimic the characters with big, energetic movements.

"'But what curse weighs on all of you on this plantation?'

"The sharpness of her voice startles the man, who didn't expect such a strong reaction.

'It's not right, Cécile, to put up with a wild child like this one,' he continues. 'She never washes. Her hair's like an rat's nest and... they say she keeps a knife hidden under her shirt....'

'Aha! You've discovered that she wears a knife under her shirt! Very well. So tell me, Canot, how is it that you discovered she was hiding this knife? From now on, she'll wear a sabre; I won't tell you again: forewarned is forearmed.'

"With his chin drawn in, the man turns an old Panama hat around and around in his hands with fingers curled up like claws, as though the words he was looking for could be found in the straw that he is crumpling nervously. He opens and closes his mouth like a fish. Canot, the Count's overseer, was born on the island, the son of a colonizer and a slave from the Plessis plantation. For a long time, he had been the man the Count relied on. Now he resents the Count since word has it that he had made one of Canot's daughters pregnant, the youngest, a fourteen-year-old. Canot ponders his bitterness and drops the subject.

"Drunk from too much sun and too many smells, in the heat that is pouring down on the plantation, the flies swirl and bump into each other, making the air deafening with their buzzing. Hitched to the hedge, Canot's mare shakes her head impatiently and seems to call him. Canot pats her tenderly on the haunches: 'There, there, my beauty, we're leaving now.'

"But Cécile plants herself right in front of Canot and threatens him with her fist.

'Do you realize, Canot, that if we were animals, we'd be treated much better?'

"Instinctively, he backs up, pulling his neck down into his shoulders. Cécile comes closer:

'If I should ever hear that one of the men on this plantation has touched a single one of Kilima's hairs—oh! I swear, seventy-seven times seven times, on the head of the woman who carried me in her womb!—this precious thing the good Lord has bequeathed you, I will cut it off and throw it to the dogs!'

"Her fists screwed to her hips, she is almost stuck to him. He smells of tobacco, of that snuff that he stuffs into his nostrils all day long.

'Look at all of you,' continues Cécile, 'more kings now than the king, more white than the whites, and why not? That's what this is all about; each of you wants to enjoy her, no?'

"A sob of anger, almost inaudible, makes her voice shake.

'Aren't you ashamed, Canot? True, I was forgetting. Your kind, with skin made for fooling the night, failed whites, failed blacks, your sort, it's true, doesn't know what shameful or unreasonable is!'

'But you know very well that it's not me, Cécile,' the man groans; I don't even see her.'

'Dear Lord,' the woman continues, 'help me, or I'll go completely mad!'

"With foam on the edge of her lips, she moves big armfuls of air. A vein quivers, like a snake that had slid into her throat.

'Doesn't she do her work as she is asked to, that Kilima? I've never seen a little black woman work harder than she does. Why do you refuse to leave her alone, you bunch of vultures? Don't you know that she still sucks her thumb at night and that milk still pearls under her nostrils? And then, damn it, good heavens, if your things can't be satisfied with what the other women on the plantation offer you, stick them in the mouths of dogs! Do you hear me, Canot? Give this advice to your black men in heat. That's right, give your things, your tools of misfortune, to the dogs. Do it with cows, horses, mares, or else, may thunder strike me down, you will have to manage with buggering each other, you bunch of pigs!'

"She turns around with such force that her head scarf falls off, revealing a mass of gray braids. Canot rushes to her feet to pick up the head scarf. She gives him a bump, a broadside of her hips as wide as a hoop, which sends the overseer rolling on the grass; then with a determined step, she walks back up the path to return to her hut.

"The Count plantation had no fewer than a hundred and fifty slaves. Cécile was both the manager of the main house and the midwife, nurse and confidante of a large number of women. She knew everything about the bush remedies that drive pain out of the body, and she knew the right words to soothe the hurts of the heart. The night after Kilima's baptism, she had gone into the hut that had been allotted to the newly arrived child and had found her prostrate as though she were dead. Her eyes were bulging out of her head and she was trembling all over. Cécile wrapped her up in her sleeping mat and led her back to her own hut. There, Cécile applied compresses of mugwort and cat's tongue to her forehead and, by inserting a spoon between her teeth, made her drink a mixture of molasses and black coffee. The moans of the child had made Cécile's blood feverish. That night was particularly trying for Cécile, who would relive her own baptism and that of her daughter, Tamu, fifteen years earlier.

"At that time, she belonged to the Plessis plantation, one of the biggest and most prosperous in the Northern Plain. She had spent twelve years there; then she'd been sold to the Count. It was the priest who had baptized her. He had given her slaps on her cheeks; then, with his big paws, hairy like spiders, he had grabbed the buttocks and breasts of the women. That sickening odour that preceded him, an indefinite mixture of alcohol, sweat, and urine, still turned her stomach, even after so many years.

"Still grumbling and cursing Canot, Cécile heads with her steady step toward the huts at the back of the garden.

'What kind of God are the whites talking about? Can anybody tell me? Spirits of the wind,' she implores, as she raises her arms, 'you who know no boundaries, who go everywhere, travel over the forests, the mountains, the valleys, rivers and oceans, ask our gods, over there, if they can understand this! Tell them to enlighten us, for pity's sake. Ask them why they've abandoned us. And these men, the ones who made the trip with us, can't even protect us any longer! What violent poisons have they been made to drink? Haven't we reached the point now where we have become prey for them as well, where we're just good enough to receive their thing, with which they pursue us in the fields during the day and into the back of our huts at night! They were told, when they were put in irons, that they were nothing but beasts; and they have ended up believing it!'

"An instinctive moan stirs in her chest, as she hurries. She thinks again about Tamu, her sweet child. She was barely twelve years old, her Tamu, with her little breasts like two pomegranate flowers, the same age as Kilima, when she was forced to sleep with this big black man, Éloi. Two children he gave her in one try, that old mastodon! Two little blacks with the eyes of a rotten fish had slid out of Tamu's belly. God of mercy! Cécile tries to hold back her sobbing.

'How many more tears must I shed, God? She is gone, my Tamu. Those demons, dead fish, gnawed at all the insides of her body. Coming back to our hut, after a day working like an animal, I discovered my Tamu...'

"Cécile swallows her tears again...

'Ah, I swear to you, Lord, you who they call the good God of this new land, on which they have thrown us like swine; listen to me, for my gods are too far away. If ever a man, whoever he may be, touches a single hair of my little Kilima, I will kill him. But no, I will kill them all, one after the other, and I will set fire to the plantation. They will pay for the harm done to Tamu. I will give them a poison that will make them all resemble the dead fish I saw come out of the belly of my Tamu. And you won't have the heart to keep me out of your paradise. Certainly not! I've toiled enough in this hell to merit that. Even with my hands covered with blood, you will have to welcome me if you are just.

'That child, Kilima, it's the gods of Guinea that took pity on my grief and sent her to me. She is all I have left of my dream and I sense that I love her like I loved my Tamu. They say that memories are kept in the heart. Ah, my own daughter! My beloved Tamu, it's here, deep down in my guts that I miss her. My heart, I no longer have one. They have torn it out of me since I can kill; I can kill whoever approaches Kilima.'"

At that point in her tale, Emma sniffles and wipes her nose for a long moment. "It was always like that," she tells me; "the women sobbed, sniffled, and rolled on the ground when they told that story.".

"When she gets back to her hut, Cécile pushes the door open, goes up to Kilima who is sleeping, takes her in her arms and then sings to her softly:

> *Kilima changu kidogo*, my little hill
> *Mkitu changu kidogo*, my little thing
> *Mtoto mdogo*, my tiny little child
> *Inakua usiku*, the night comes
> *Wewe malayika wangu*, my guardian angel

"Almost two years had passed since Kilima had arrived on the plantation. Her face had miraculously kept its roundness; and her little dimples seemed deeper. Her pupils, on the other hand, had lost all their sparkle.

"Cécile, who had adopted her, had pleaded her case before the Count, begging him to give the child, who seemed fragile, domestic work in the great house. She had praised Kilima's docility, her good behaviour, and her obedience. Nothing had made the master give in.

'She is already a real bargain, your Kilima, believe me,' belched the Count. 'A beautiful rump, for true. She has solid arms and legs; and I have been told that she puts fifty armfuls of cane into bundles in the blink of an eye. Everything considered, I don't know if it's a good idea that she still be in your hut, Cécile. You won't be able to keep her forever under your wing. Am I God, that I should be feeding and housing people out of the goodness of my heart who are not as useful as they should be on my property?'

'Take care not to take the name of God in vain, Sir. Up there where He is, if He hears you, He wouldn't like that at all.'

'Your age and your status as an elder on this property are not a guarantee of your impunity, Cécile. Beware.'

"The Count was standing. His hands were moving back and forth on his paunch. He had just gotten up from the dinner table, the same table that Cécile was leaning over as she was busy cleaning it off. He let out a loud belch, followed by a bestial chuckle, then he reached out his arm as though to seize the woman. Quickly, she picked up the serving knife, whose blade was still glistening with grease. The prominent forehead of the Count wrinkled in astonishment. His long jaw, his hooked nose, his whole physique revealed an insatiable being, a caricature of a man that power and lust had transformed into a monster.

'It's out of necessity that you didn't send me to the fields with the others,' she shot at him, 'because I run the house like no one else here could do it. But in spite of all these years spent under your roof, you still know absolutely nothing about me, sir. In my veins flows the bitterest venom. One more step and you will learn very quickly what this venom is worth. Me, I have already seen everything, known everything in this life, including the hell of being under your roof. I am not looking for anything, I don't need anything. Consider carefully, between you and me, who has the most to lose?'

"The woman was now rolling white eyes; a convulsive trembling was starting to spread throughout her body. A moment of truth? The house suddenly seemed so large and empty to the Count, alone with that woman armed with a long knife. A sinister vision of his guts, dangling out of his white belly, of his gashed body over which a horde of blacks is squabbling, took the place of the obsessive vision that had lingered in him for a long time, that of his hands buried in that mass of tobacco-coloured flesh, of his fingers kneading the flabby breasts, of her vagina, overcoming without consideration the presumptuousness of that slave, much younger than she claimed. He threw her a last, undecipherable look, then, without a word, hastily left the room, telling himself that he'd have to think of a way to get rid of her."

Dr. MacLeod had long since left the room on tiptoe. Emma, I believe, did not even notice; she didn't interrupt her tale. Time had been turned back long before; I no longer existed. Nor did Emma. In the hut with the walls painted a green colour, there were now Kilima, Cécile, and Béa.

"The evening was well along when Cécile got back to Kilima. It had rained all afternoon. The sour smell of the soaked straw of the roof filled the hut.

"As on every evening for the previous two years, Cécile found the little girl curled up in the most obscure corner of the hut. In the muffled and suffocating buzzing of the silence, motionless, the child was on the alert, listening for the slightest noise. Her laboured breathing guided Cécile toward her. As she was vigorously rubbing the child, Cécile grumbled:

'In good weather, in bad weather, she's buffeted by the gusts, drenched by the showers, cooked and re-cooked by the sun; that's what makes her sick. That exhausting work in the fields doesn't suit such a delicate creature.'

"Every evening, on the threshold of her hut, Cécile discarded the sea swell that, all day long, had accompanied her in the white great house, stirred her up, made her arms active, her hands agile, and her feet move from the basement up to the attic. In the mud in front of her hut, she buried until the next day that rage—a resistance to despair and destruction—which was much stronger than she realized. She would then rediscover this completely unprecedented desire to live which was growing in her, brought by this child, now welded to her pain. By dint of patience, love, and gentle fibs, she had eventually gotten through to the heart of the little girl. On certain nights, full of so many evocations, so many murmured words and secrets, sleep deserted the hut. From the rubble of her ravaged memory, Cécile picked out the slender little lifelines that she held out to Kilima, teaching her, night after night, the path of revolt.

"The voice of the woman reached the child as though it was coming from another place, another body. A voice whispered by the wind, whose spirit knew neither flooding rivers, nor high mountains, nor dense forests.

> *Kilima changu kidogo*, my little hill
> *Kitu changu kidogo*, my little thing
> *Mtoto mdogo*, my tiny little child
> *Inakua usiku*, the night comes
> *Wewe malayika wangu*, my guardian angel

"After giving the child a rubdown and serving her the leftovers of the meal that she brought back from the great house, she asked Kilima to undo her braids for her.

'That helps me to put a little order in there, my child,' she said, full of gratitude, as she tapped her skull with sharp little blows.

"Sometimes, burying her face in the crackling mass of the child's uncombed hair, she washed it with her tears.

'The tears of women, it's like their milk, Kilima my angel. They never dry up. The more we shed, the more there are. And it can happen that they are as good as milk, you know.'

"In a fierce tone, the child would protest:

'Not me, I won't cry. No, never. I know something that can drive away tears for good. I know something, it's inside me, mama, and I don't know its name. I don't know the word, mama; my tongue doesn't know the word; so... perhaps there is no word for it.'

"She fell into a panic, squeezed her fists; and her eyes seemed to wander.

Kitu changu kidogo, my little thing
Mtoto mdogo, my tiny little child

'Be calm, my child,' Cécile told her. 'You mustn't get too attached to words, or have too much confidence in them. Often, in our mouths, they are like specks of dust spinning in dizzy confusion across a ray of light. So they go mad; they don't know what they are saying anymore.

Kitu changu kidogo, my little thing
Mtoto mdogo, my tiny little child

'Lots of things stay in our guts forever; because we don't know how to express them, they remain nameless. But they are so alive inside us. Sometimes we know them so well we have the impression that we could simply point a finger to show the exact place where we feel them quiver or boil. Other times we remember them like our ears remember a cry. Me, I prefer the things that don't yet have a name, those that we remember all the time and for which we don't need a name. It's that way for Tamu,' Cécile said to Kilima. 'Her absence has no name. Her absence is a cry. Like the call of a bird. That's it, like a bird, with its head extended forward; she left us, like the bird that nosedives in a final fluttering of wings. And she had puffed so much, and screamed so much, her skin glistened with so much sweat and all her hair was glued to her face, like a wet bird. That's how it feels, like a cry. But then didn't it happen that you arrived, my child! Ah, I promise you that they will never dare touch you as long as I'm alive.'

"The season had poured an atrocious heat on the island. The maddened insects swirled without respite in the humid air, filling it with a furious buzzing. Not one ounce of gray in the sky; blue, everywhere a blinding blue. Barely ten in the morning, and already the sun seemed to want to pulverize the hills that surrounded the property. All around, the crackling of the dried-up plants added to the anguish. The harvests had been bad, the rains not abundant enough. On the plantation, people were in a murderous mood, all the more so since a rumour from who knows where had it that the Count was preparing to shake up all the field work.

"He had come back from a trip to the south of the island, during which he had made a purchase of slaves and some new livestock. A few attempts at revolt in the plantations down there had been brutally crushed. He had been able to see for himself that his colleagues in the south had truly earned their reputation for being tough. Those guys certainly didn't go easy on their blacks like he did on his. The captured rebels whose ears—one from some, two from others—had been cut off, had afterward become harder workers. His southern colleagues had assured him that he had made a good deal by acquiring several of them.

"Cécile was on the alert. She saw the Count arrive and, with his self-satisfied swagger, approach the overseer.

'Hello, Canot,' said the Count, getting off his horse.

'You are back long before you planned, Sir.'

"The master's only answer was to hand him the bridle and order him to water his horse.

"It didn't matter where the overseer was on the immense property, he could always guess when the Count was coming. He would then come running over to him, cutting across the fields, winded, tripping on the stones, his hat in his hand.

'Canot,' the Count started, swaying backwards and forwards, 'I've discovered that the colonizers in the South have a much firmer hand than I do. I should send you down there so you can see how they would treat this bunch of idlers.'

'Without wanting to contradict you, Sir,' Canot answered immediately, 'I know from a reliable source that on the Guibert plantation the master preferred to bring up an overseer from a plantation in the South. Perhaps that would be better, Sir. You would have all that at your disposal. You have to do it yourself if you want it done right, as you tell us all the time. Me, I am already too old to adopt new ways of doing things. But I can tell you that rumours of an uprising are erupting everywhere on the plantation, Sir, I can assure you of that.'

"The overseer had spoken, it seemed, with the same deference due to the white man that he usually showed. But, the tone of his voice made the master realize that something wasn't quite right.

'If rumours of this kind are running around the plantation, it's because someone is not doing his work as he should, Canot.'

"Having dismissed Canot with the back of his hand, the Count thought to himself: 'that conversation took a bad turn....' He turned his back on him and, with a heavy step, had started to climb the steps leading to the great house. Changing his mind, he turned around and called to him:

'Canot? Find me Cécile, and tell her to send back that little black girl immediately, you know, the one who insists that we call her Kilima; Cécile should send her back to her own hut, the one that was assigned to her when she arrived here. It must be done by this evening, with no more delay. It is time they learn who's the master here.'

"That evening, we were on the porch, Mattie and I. The story of Kilima was a long time in coming," Emma recalls. "It was another one of those nights of booming drums and blazing heat. We didn't sleep, Mattie and I. 'There are nights for this,' Mattie would say sometimes. 'When time goes too fast, you have to know how to lengthen it, even to trick it, hide from it, my little Emma.'

"Mattie had suspended her narrative, as though she was holding a thread between her fingers. Her eyes were travelling far in the distance. Abruptly, as though she felt cold, she tightened around her neck an old shawl that she never took off, a relic. The wind whistled as it dodged in and out between the metal sheets and the beams of the porch.

'But what happened, Mattie? Kilima, did she go to her own hut?' I asked her.

"My voice reminds Mattie that I am there, at her side, that this tale from long ago was given to her so that she could transmit it to me. For the length of a caress, her hand moves over my cheek.

'All that comes from very far away, Emma,' she tells me, suddenly flustered by the fright that is evident on my face. 'All that comes from very far away. There are those of us who claim that our stories are only legends. They would claim anything in order to banish this period from their memory. To camouflage the insult, we have made it a practice to construct legends, like one builds cathedrals, or we retreat into silence.'

'I know the true reason for the silences, Mattie,' I confided to her gently. 'The reason they never mention. It's somewhere deep down inside us, between discretion and secrecy. No one talks about it because it's too shameful, too hurtful. We don't talk about it because doing so reminds us of the long ago days, the days of the whip and the insult... That's one of the reasons why the teacher and other girls detest me. I wrote a composition on that period.

'I explained that we prefer silence as a way of pretending to have forgotten. When we discover this secret, we are aghast, I wrote. We are there like witnesses and we feel smothered by shame. Then we try to find the pieces that escape us, as though it was about some clothing made from rags. Sometimes I tell myself that perhaps the words don't exist to tell of that shame. That's what it is. These are things for which there are no words.'

'But the story of Kilima is the real truth,' said Mattie. 'There is no silence that can keep it quiet, no silence that could manage to erase it from our memories.'

"Kilima did not return to the hut that she had been assigned to. The next day, the Count enter-

tained at dinner his colleagues from the neighbouring plantations. The rum was flowing. He
required that little Kilima wait on them as naked
as a worm, naked as the day she was born.

"When night came, three of them entered
the hut. Tired from the heavy work of her day,
Cécile had dozed off. Kilima's scream woke her
up. Jumping up, she thrust her hand under her
mattress and seized a long knife. She drove it up
to the handle into the back of the Count, who
collapsed. The two others grabbed Cécile; they
cut off her hands and feet. Then they seized
Kilima and cut off her nose, telling her: 'From
now on, no one will look at you.' This was a
mutilation that was reserved mainly for women.
That night on the plantation, madness was very
much alive, present, real.

"Kilima, with the help of a few slaves, spread
gasoline throughout the plantation and set fire
to it. Then, they fled into the hills carrying
Cécile with them. Later, Kilima gave birth to a
daughter whom she attempted to drown; after
that she went mad. One day, dressed completely in white, she walked into the ocean and never
came back. She had returned to the route of the
big boats. As for Cécile, for many years she was
the leader of a group of slaves. She walked with
the help of her stumps; and with the help of her
mouth, she succeeded in handling a musket as
well as the most highly skilled soldier.

'And the Count, did he die, really die that day?' I asked Mattie; for, in my opinion, it was necessary that he expiate, that he pay for, his crime.

'That is not important,' she had answered me. 'One day,' she said finally, 'a day will come when you will understand that life never readily offers up its truths. One has to learn to patiently question existence, to decipher it, like a dream, like an unknown alphabet... When my answers aren't enough for you, you'll have to find them for yourself.'

"I savoured those moments with Mattie, but I felt already rising in me a burning revolt, like the lava of a volcano. Sometimes I cried. My nights were peopled with nightmares.

"You know, Flore, sometimes I call on Kilima, Cécile, the Emmas before me, then Rosa, all those eternal maroons, for help. I invoke their memory; they will know how to guide me, I tell myself; but I don't see them. Often, I look at the river in the hope of seeing them appear. At night, I go to bed very early, to return to my dreams and my grandmother, Rosa. But the dreams shun me, Flore, ever since I have been confined here. I don't dream anymore. I don't dream anymore at all. By confining me here, they have really managed to steal my soul."

The hours pass one after the other; night has fallen on the river; I haven't left Emma. I can't bring myself to leave. Since she stays calm when I am there, the nurses don't say anything, more than happy not to hear the screams of the negro lady in 122. It will soon be midnight, and Emma is still talking:

"Almost two centuries after the arrival of my ancestor Kilima, I left that island where the sweat of blacks had fertilized the fields of cotton, tobacco, sugar cane and indigo to build capitals and fortunes for the Old World. Ah, if stones could talk, Flore! If the dirty water of the ports, which has lapped for centuries against the voracious planks of the slave ships that returned stuffed with gold, spices, sugar, and rum; if that water, infected with the lure of lucre that thrilled the approaches to the docks of Cadiz, Nantes, and Bordeaux, could only talk...

"I left that island which had known centuries of cut-off feet and arms, of torn-off ears. On the eve of my departure," Emma continues sadly, "I walked for a long time. I took the road that goes down to the port to look at the sea. All this blue for nothing. I thought about the boats, about all those ships that the slave traders had sunk with thousands of slaves chained in their holds. They sank the ships to avoid being caught, to avoid paying a fine, when laws had finally been adopted to try to prohibit slavery. But it was too late.

The worm was in the fruit. The hate and scorn that had been practiced toward women whose skin was the colour of night had already swollen in them up to their bosoms.

"All this past is past in name only, Flore. It continues to remain there, lying in wait for us, behind the obscure fog of forgetfulness. That's where my decision to study the history of slavery comes from. But you already know what they did to me. They refused to hear my voice. All I wanted was to write this book that, whenever it was opened, would never ever be closed. But you already know everything.

"They claim that time manages to heal the deepest wounds. How many centuries will it take to close up these wounds? The early morning gray of October which welcomed me to Bordeaux didn't give me any sign of how much time I would need to heal. The immigration officer had the look, both empty and piercing, of an official, well-trained to look without seeing. He turned the pages of my passport indifferently. Then, with a limp hand, he pointed to the long corridor.

"At the end of the corridor, no one was waiting for me.

"Is it possible to be cured of the hate and scorn that we have been swallowing in strong doses ever since the beginning of the world?"

These words are the last ones that I gathered from Emma's mouth.

They made their way into me, never to leave me. I feel them, like living things that swell, burst into a thousand little pains, gather in the pit of my stomach. Sometimes they settle near my heart and create in me an infinite uneasiness. At other times, they calm me.

The Route of the Big Boats

It was a morning in the month of May; it must have been seven o'clock. The telephone had started to ring. The ringing continued, but I didn't get up to answer it. I was exhausted by the recent weeks spent transcribing what Dr. MacLeod calls "Emma's obsessive delirium" as well as by the lack of compassion shown by the doctor who, in my opinion, had lost all interest in his patient.

For Dr. MacLeod, Emma was no longer a human being, but a case, a file, perhaps even an object in room 122. He had eventually taken my sense of responsibility to Emma for granted. There was nothing abnormal for him about the fact that I was left alone to carry the burden of her terrifying tale, alone to listen to her, to talk to her, to offer her my friendship. During the long days that I was meeting with her in the hospital, in her little room with the green walls, the telephone had never rung for her, no one called her. The only flowers that she ever received were the ones that I had thought to bring her.

Where were her friends? I sometimes wondered. All those people that she must have known during her many years as a student? And that man, Nickolas, why had she banished him from her existence? The mystery would remain unsolved, for I never dared to approach her about it.

That day, I was thinking about going to the hospital a little ahead of time. Something that I couldn't put my finger on was troubling me. As usual, I had telephoned to request that Emma be informed that I was coming. The operator told me simply that the patient in room 122 was no longer there.

"It's for Ms. Bratte," I insisted. "I am Flore, the interpreter; I work with Dr. MacLeod."

"I know," continued the woman at the end of the line with much impatience in her voice. "She is no longer there. I will connect you with the nursing station."

"We telephoned you around seven o'clock this morning, Flore," the nurse told me; "no one answered. Dr. MacLeod and the police want to see you; the patient in room 122 has committed suicide."

I put down the receiver and rushed to the bathroom, where I vomited my guts out. In the mirror, I didn't recognize myself. I opened my eyes wide, as though I was suddenly in the middle of a thick fog. I heard Emma's voice murmuring: "That curse from the holds of the slave ships is such that the very womb that carried us can crush us. And the flesh of your own flesh transforms itself into a fanged beast and eats you up from within. That's why Lola needed to die. What did it matter, now or later; what did it matter? Like me, Lola was condemned." That is all she had ever said on the subject of the murder of her daughter.

Two weeks earlier, Dr. MacLeod had told her that he would soon be finishing his report and making his recommendations. There would be no trial, he said. In his opinion, she had been unfit to stand trial. Emma had said the contrary. She had prepared her defense by herself, out of her desire to confront the judges and put a bit of sense in the brains of the journalists. "They have written so much garbage, so much nonsense," she had moaned. "In spite of all their great books, they are ignoramuses."

W hat should the police be told; in what terms should I talk to them about Emma? There they were, three strapping men in impeccable suits, three strong men, virile and armed. Dr.

MacLeod, the one Emma called "Little Doctor," truly seemed very small in his immaculate white coat. It's funny, I told myself, I had never noticed that he was cross-eyed and that he had so much hair in his nostrils and his ears. His ears are particularly large; and their redness accentuates their size. What has he learned from Emma's life?

I wasn't listening to what the policemen were saying; I wasn't listening to anything. They were standing in front of me, but I hardly saw them. As though through a window, they seemed to me to be far away, fugitive shadows, carrying away with them a carcass, Emma's body. What did they all want from me, for the love of God? What to do when death scorns us, when it laughs with the guttural laugh, full of irony and pain, that escaped from Emma's belly?

If Emma had hung herself, they would have said that I had provided her with the rope. A guilty party, that always suits everyone. But nothing was settled because the guilty party was the river. How could this have happened? No one knew. All the doors were locked, but she had gotten out nevertheless. She had walked along the bank, dressed in her white dress. She had put on her mauve turban that made her look like a madonna. They had found the dress; it was floating on the water, and the skirt was puffed up like a jellyfish.

"She always said, she said repeatedly, that she would return to the route of the big boats." That's how I responded to the policeman, the tall blond one with a mustache that danced with each of his words.

"She hasn't been here for a long time," I continued, when he thought it useful to ask me if I had been able to observe any sign indicating that she was planning to commit suicide. "Her soul has returned to the river to make the return trip."

Hearing these words, one of the policemen swallowed his chewing gum and started coughing. Staring at me with a stern look, he asked me to repeat what I had just said. I repeated, for the pleasure of hearing my voice: "Emma often told me that one day she would go back to the route of the big boats to join the others."

Raising his eyebrows, the policeman turned toward Dr. MacLeod. Unfortunately for the officer, I understood what he was indicating with his facial expression and his language. "Another one who is losing her mind," he wanted to imply. But they won't get the better of me. I ask them politely if they've finished. I am not a social worker, or a psychologist, or an employee of the hospital. I offer my services as an interpreter. I got attached to the patient. Through solidarity... because of our blood... that same blood...

They had just come from Nickolas Zankoffi's place. They had questioned him. They wanted to see the apartment; they had gone into the bedroom and had read the words Emma had written hanging on the wall opposite the bed.

They asked me if I understood what she had meant. I shrugged my shoulders. I heard Emma's voice: 'A woman who talks too much makes as much noise as a cloud, Flore. It's sometimes better to swallow one's tongue.'

What did it mean to them? I didn't ask.

Just like on the day that Dr. MacLeod had invited me to work with him on Emma's case, I wandered aimlessly about the city. I didn't want to call Gilliane or Mother. I didn't want to call anyone; no one would have understood. The luminous intensity of the daylight was hurting me. Everything was hurting me. I cursed the whole universe. I cursed Gilliane who would have said that Emma was a condemned woman, whatever the outcome. Some sirens were wailing; what were they announcing? Emma's death. No. No one was announcing her death. She wasn't dead; she had joined the others, over there. I was walking, repeating::"life can't be just that; it's too stupid." I wanted to be a man, to go into a bar and invite a woman to come home with me, to drown myself in her body. I wanted to be a bird, a cat... to exist no longer, to think no longer.

I found myself suddenly in front of the old building where Nickolas lived. I rang the buzzer; he opened the door and I threw myself into his arms. I didn't understand anything, neither what I was looking for, nor what I wanted. An instant later, I felt his hand in mine, then I felt it slide over my body. All I remember is gasping for air with a voracious despair, like in a shipwreck, and yelling as if I had lost my mind, an unending yell to expel, finally, all that horror. Then I felt myself falling, falling, sliding, capsizing, and dying.

That night, just as one loves in order to cure the soul and the body, like a balm that one spreads over a wound, Nickolas loved me. Somewhere between madness, desire, and passion, I no longer knew who I was. Nickolas no longer knew which body he was kissing. He was drinking an unloved body, the body of all black women. He was making love to them to defeat all the eternities when love had been missing for them. Burning pleasure, wet and warm, my body was that of Emma. Flore, Nickolas, two beings adrift, drowning their grief in a sudden fantasy. We were sailing on an unknown ocean. Would it be possible to return unscathed from such a trip? It was immense, magical; it was too much for me. I squeezed my temples to force out the words that stopped somewhere in me, halfway between madness and reason. Who is it that wrote that desire and suffering are Siamese twins? I tried desperately to evade that embrace, to pull myself away from Nickolas. I wanted to tell him that it wasn't possible. And I thought about Emma's words, about the curse on our blood that ran under my skin and deep down in my pupils made to fool the night. Who then was I being unfaithful to? I asked myself, panic stricken: the memory of Emma, my boredom, my dismay, or this man? I slowly opened my mouth; I hesitated, the sounds weren't leaving my lips. That man is an enchanter, Flore; nevermore will you be able to live without him. Nevermore?

"Emma-Flore-Emma," he repeated, while the voice of Emma whispered: "They have always taught us that love, like everything which is good on this earth, isn't made for us."

Emma. Wasn't she there, guiding over my body the body of that man, guiding me, one of the few to have patiently learned her language? Yes, I told myself, Emma is bringing me into the world; she is reinventing my birth. She is there to lead her last fight and to defeat destiny, through me.

The bed, was it a ship, a slave ship? Who

was that man? Where was he leading me? Feeling faint, I opened my eyes and found Emma, at my side. She was staring at me, just like on the first day in the room with the green walls in the hospital. What did it mean, Emma's immobile gaze, the statue-like gaze of her narrow face? At that moment I felt an irresistible urge to hug her, while from the deepest part of my being an elation sprang up that emptied me out and filled me up, compelling me to think no more, to desire nothing more than this brief instant, this body against mine. But Emma's eyes, glued to me, told me the contrary: "Breathe in his scent with pleasure; learn to nest in the curve of his arm, to let your body be impregnated with the memory of that swell; quite simply, learn that you are first a woman and then a black woman."